Not Like the Others

Bart watched her, then realized he was staring at her. She was so pretty it almost took his breath away. Holly Daniels. Her name fit her perfectly — she looked pure and fresh.

He couldn't believe he had never seen her before. How could he have been in the same building with her for the past six weeks without noticing her? But then, it was a big school, and the people he knew were either part of his crowd, in his classes, or on the football team. The other girls he knew were ones who let him know they were there — like Heather, or Kristi Marshall — the ones who obviously wanted something from him. This girl, he could tell immediately, wasn't anything like that.

WHAT EVERY GIRL WANTS MOST OF ALL – TO BE PART OF A COUPLE!

BY LINDA A. COONEY

Meet the couples and couples-to-be at Kennedy High School in this thrilling new series – pretty Chris and athletic Ted, popular Phoebe and serious Brad, the dreamy Griffin and cool D. J. Peter, plain Janie and vampy Lauri, sensitive Woody and troubled, troublesome Brenda. Follow them through their first loves, break-ups and crushes – the joys and pitfalls, the attractions and the special moments.

One new title every month! Available wherever Bantam paperbacks are sold.

COMING SOON . . .
COUPLES SPECIAL EDITION
SUMMER HEAT!

COMING ON STRONG

by M.E. Cooper

BANTAM BOOKS

TORONTO • NEW YORK • LONDON • SYDNEY • AUCKLAND

For Andrea Warren

COMING ON STRONG

A BANTAM BOOK   0 553 17469 X

Produced by Cloverdale Press Inc.,
133 Fifth Avenue, New York, NY10003
Bantam Edition Published 1987

Reproduced, printed and bound in Great Britain by
Hazell Watson & Viney Limited,
Member of the BPCC Group,
Aylesbury, Bucks

Chapter
1

Holly Daniels sighed as she looked through the sweaters stacked in her bottom drawer. When she got her next paycheck, she definitely owed herself a trip to the Rose Hill Mall to buy one or two new ones. Today was perfect for a light-weight sweater — it was a crisp, sunny October day — and she didn't have a single one.

She continued to dig through the pile, and then she remembered the soft, aqua-colored cashmere her father and stepmother had given her for Christmas last year. It was just right for today. How could she have forgotten about it?

She touched the softness of the sleeve to her cheek and stood up, holding the sweater in front of her as she eyed it critically in the mirror.

Perfect! She would wear it over her pale yellow blouse with her white pinstriped jeans. She co-ordinated her outfit with care since this morning she would be attending Ms. Tyler's economics discussion group for the first time, and first impressions counted with teachers.

What a pain to have to transfer sections six weeks into the school year — and just when she was getting used to a new school — but at least the office had approved her application for a work release on Tuesday and Thursday afternoons, and economics had been the only class she'd needed to switch.

It was nice to be back in Rose Hill, where she had been born and had lived until the end of sixth grade, when her parents had divorced. She and her mother had moved to Baltimore. Last summer her mother had been offered a good job in Rose Hill, and they had moved back just in time for the beginning of a new school year.

Starting as a junior in a new school was scary, but Kennedy was so much better than the school Holly had been attending that she was glad to be there. The kids were very nice and she already was starting to make some friends.

She studied her reflection in the full-length mirror. The sweater's color set off her hazel eyes and short, curly brown hair. She eyed her slim legs and wished, as she always did, that they were longer, but since she was only five foot four, what could she expect?

Her favorite Bruce Springsteen song came onto the radio and she danced around her room, pulling on her clothes, singing along, her low, husky voice blending in with his.

Just as she finished dressing, the phone next to her bed rang. She heard her mother answer it in the kitchen, and a moment later she called down the hall, "It's for you, Holly, it's Dr. Ellerbee."

"Thanks, Mom." She frowned. If Dr. E. was phoning this early, it had to be because he wanted her to work tonight — and tonight was a Kennedy High–Leesburg Academy football game.

"I hate to ask, Holly," Dr. Ellerbee began after saying hello. Her heart sank, knowing what was coming. "We need you to work tonight. We're going to be short-handed because June still has the flu, and Susan is out of town."

She knew she couldn't say no. Since she was only a junior in high school, he had gone out on a limb giving her a part-time job as an aide at the medical clinic of the Rose Hill Hospital, where he was director. She had talked him into taking a chance on her and she was working hard to prove she was worthy of it.

The clinic served as an emergency room for the surrounding area and as a walk-in doctor's office. Holly helped with a wide range of routine procedures, as well as with medical emergencies, and when things got busy, she got to spend far more time with patients than she ever would have working in a regular hospital or helping out in a doctor's office.

She had been working part-time since school started, and Dr. Ellerbee had recently increased her hours on Tuesday and Thursday afternoons — which was why she was switching economics classes. She also worked a flexible schedule but had asked for the night off so she could attend the game.

"I'm sorry you'll have to miss the football

3

game," Dr. Ellerbee continued. "You can leave at ten when Alice comes instead of staying until midnight. Until then, it'll just be you, and me, Cheryl, and Steven Ewing."

Holly perked up when she heard Steven's name. He was a good-looking pre-med student from Georgetown University who worked part-time at the clinic. He had thick dark brown hair, huge brown eyes, and was very tall. He had grown up in Brooklyn and Holly loved to hear his accent, which she found exotic. They had only worked the same shift twice before, but both times he had been friendly and talkative.

Holly was sure that he liked her. She hoped so, because she liked him. He was hard-working and ambitious, as well as cute, and he knew exactly what he wanted from life and was willing to make sacrifices to get it. That appealed to her.

"Okay, I'll see you at six, Dr. E.," she said.

When she walked into the kitchen, her mother was getting ready to leave for work. She smiled at Holly. "Let me guess. You have to work tonight, right? We'll have an early supper, then I have a date with Bruce, so I'll be going out, too."

Holly laughed at the matter-of-fact way her mother had slipped in this last information. "*Another* date with Bruce? Hmmm. This is starting to sound serious," she teased.

Holly knew her mother really liked Bruce. He was a pharmacist who had come to the dental office where her mother worked a month ago to have his teeth cleaned and had called back the next day to ask her out to dinner. They had seen each other steadily ever since.

"There's fresh juice in the fridge and I got some bagels at the bakery last night if you want one," her mother said, looking through her purse for her car keys. "Anything special going on at school today?"

"A math quiz, and I'm switching econ small groups and I start the new section today," Holly answered, splitting open a bagel and spreading it with butter. "Since I won't be going to the football game tonight, I guess that's about it."

Her mother opened the door, then turned to kiss Holly good-bye. She drew back, frowning. "Is that the sweater your father and his wife gave you last Christmas?"

Holly nodded. She suddenly remembered why she had put the sweater at the back of her drawer, underneath the others.

"Well, it looks very nice. You should wear it more often."

Surprised by this unexpected compliment, Holly smiled at her mother, who was already walking out the door. She stepped outside and waved as her mother drove away.

Maybe her mother's romance with Bruce was helping her to get over the bitterness she had felt when Holly's dad had remarried three years earlier and moved to Los Angeles. She had had trouble accepting the fact that Holly liked her stepmother, and looked forward to seeing her and her father each summer when she went to visit them.

It was odd having a mother who dated. Sometimes Holly felt like her mother's mother, trying to keep track of where she was going and with

5

whom. It wouldn't surprise her if her mother decided to marry Bruce. That would be fine with her; he was a friendly guy who acted as if he really cared for her mother. It would mean she could start thinking about the best nursing schools to apply to instead of concentrating just on the ones in the area. She wouldn't have to worry about her mother being lonely if she remarried.

She glanced at her watch. She still had twenty minutes before she had to leave for school, time enough for a quick review for her math quiz.

Absently chewing on her bagel, she got out her math book, then realized that she had left the review sheet for the quiz in her notebook at school. Was it all of chapter fourteen, or just the last section? She couldn't remember. A phone number on the inside cover of her book caught her eye. It was Diana Einerson's, the girl who sat next to her in math. She and Diana were getting to be pretty good friends.

Diana was also new at Kennedy High, a junior transfer student from Montana. But Diana was already so settled in at school that you'd never know she hadn't always lived there. Her father was a congressman. Her brother Bart was a senior at Kennedy High and on the football team, and Diana was going out with Jeremy Stone, a student from England who had a wonderful British accent. Diana had also become part of *the* crowd at Kennedy, while Holly was still learning her way around and getting to know people.

If Holly hadn't moved away from Rose Hill, she might have been part of that crowd, too. In fifth and sixth grades she had been best friends with Phoebe Hall, now a vivacious senior at Kennedy and at the center of the crowd. Holly had lived doors away from Phoebe then, but after the divorce she and her mother had moved to Baltimore, and they hadn't kept in touch.

Holly had seen Phoebe at school a few times since September, but they were both always on their way somewhere, and besides a quick hello, they hadn't talked at all. The next time she saw Phoebe, she would suggest that they get together some day after school. She was certain she would like Phoebe as much as she had all those years ago.

On the other hand, maybe it wasn't such a good idea. She knew she and Phoebe had drifted into different worlds since then. Now Phoebe had friends like Chris Austin, the president of the student council, and Sasha Jenkins, the editor of the school paper.

Probably none of them had to have part-time jobs like Holly did just to buy clothes or keep their cars running. She and her mother now lived in a modest two-bedroom house, far from the shady streets of beautiful homes where Phoebe and most of her friends lived.

She dialed the number in her book and Diana answered on the first ring. "Hi, Holly," she said, her voice cheerful, "isn't it great out today?"

Diana had a natural quality that Holly loved. There was nothing artificial about her; she was friendly and easy to talk to. Not like some of the girls at Kennedy whose fathers were important government officials or successful businessmen — girls like Heather Richardson, who made sure everyone knew that her father was Douglas Richardson of the State Department, and loved to flaunt her family's wealth. But then, Diana came from Montana, and had lived on a ranch all her life until her father was elected to Congress. Maybe it was the ranch life that had made her so down-to-earth. Sometimes she seemed almost shy. She was pretty, too, but in an unpretentious way, as though she herself didn't know it.

"I can hardly wait for the game tonight," Diana continued. "Bart's excited, too. He's here in the kitchen eating up a storm."

Holly laughed. "I thought football players got so nervous they couldn't eat on game days."

"Bart could eat *anything any* time," Diana said sarcastically. "Gale winds could be blowing down the house and he'd be in the kitchen making a sandwich."

Holly heard Diana's brother protesting in the background. "Hey!" he laughed. "Don't give away any family secrets!"

Holly knew who Bart Einerson was. The first time she had seen him was when all of the football players had been introduced at the first pep rally of the year. She had since seen him around school. He was hard not to notice because he was tall, dark, and had a rugged, handsome face. He was also outgoing, and extremely friendly, especially to girls.

Holly knew the kind of boy he was — a flirt with a devastating smile who came on to all the girls he knew and then never got involved with a single one. Nothing like a serious Steven.

She reviewed the math assignment with Diana

and when they were about to hang up, Diana said, "Let's sit together at the football game tonight. Jeremy'll be taking pictures, so he'll be down on the sidelines, and — "

"Thanks," Holly interrupted, disappointed, "but I just found out I have to work tonight. Maybe next week — *if* I don't have to work."

"Too bad you have to miss the game," Diana said sympathetically. "But okay, I'll plan on sitting with you next week. Gotta go. I hear Jeremy's car out front. See you in math."

Holly hung up the phone and smiled to herself. She had the feeling she and Diana were going to become good friends. Lots of good things were happening — her job, Steven, Diana, her mother's happiness. Being back in Rose Hill was turning out much better than she had expected.

She put her math papers away, put her dishes in the sink, and loaded her backpack with books. The smile was still on her face as she walked out the door, locking it behind her.

Chapter
2

Bart Einerson glanced to his right as Ted Mason expertly maneuvered his tiny red MG into a parking space in the student lot. "Hey, Mason, what's going on over there?" Bart asked, motioning to a carload of girls in a burgundy BMW pulling into the adjoining space.

Ted laughed. "Junior groupies. They've been following us. They like senior football players, especially on the day of the most important game of the year, so watch out."

Bart smiled at the blonde girl in the driver's seat and she gave him an appreciative smile back. As he got out of the car, she quickly opened her door and stepped out, blocking his way. "Oops! Sorry," she purred. From the backseat, one of her girl friends began to giggle. "You're Bart Einerson, aren't you?" she said flirtatiously, her body close to his. "I saw you play last week. You were incredible! I can't *wait* to see you in action against Leesburg tonight."

Bart smiled, his blue eyes casually checking her out. She was wearing a pep squad uniform, only her sweater looked a little tighter and her skirt a little shorter than the other girls'. She had a good figure, nice face, and a classy car. "It's nice to know someone in the stands notices," he said. "You're — "

"Heather. Heather Richardson." She emphasized her last name. "My father is Douglas Richardson of the State Department. I'm sure you've heard of him." She lightly touched the sleeve of his jacket. "And *your* father is Representative Donald Einerson, isn't he? I saw him on the news. He's so handsome!"

Bart nodded, his square jaw tightening. And *so* busy, he wanted to say. Back home, he and his father had run the family ranch almost as a team. But since the move to Washington, his father was so busy with his duties as Montana's junior congressman that the rest of the family barely saw him.

"Good luck tonight," Heather cooed, finally moving aside just enough so Bart could slide past her. He grinned at her, his even white teeth setting off his tanned skin. He ran a hand through his dark hair, then waved as he hurried after Ted, who was already halfway across the parking lot. "See you around," he called.

"I *hope* so," she said. "I'd *like* that." Her girl friends immediately gathered around her, complimenting her on her technique, as they walked in a tight group toward the school.

Ahead of them, Bart caught up with Ted, who was laughing and shaking his head. "I don't know how you do it, Einerson. You're like a magnet to girls. Heather Richardson's obviously got plans for you."

"You know her?" Bart asked, falling into step beside him.

Ted shrugged. "I know her slightly. She's not my type, a little *too* aggressive, if you know what I mean." He glanced at Bart. "But you do seem to have a magic touch. I've seen the girls swarming around you in the cafeteria."

Bart grinned. "There's nothing to it. I'll give you lessons if you want. *The Fine Art of Picking Up Girls* by Bart Einerson. Chapter One: Never miss an opportunity to flirt with anyone good-looking."

"I wasn't saying I needed your pointers. I was only stating a fact."

"Sorry, Ted, I forgot."

Ted stopped at the entrance to the school and leaned against the stone stoop. Bart stopped beside him, feeling the warmth of the early morning sun on the back of his neck. He could see the pain in his friend's face and he knew he was thinking about Molly. Ted had met Molly Ramirez at the beach last summer and had fallen head-over-heels in love with her. They had experienced a brief, intense romance before Molly went home to California at the end of August, and Ted had not been in touch with her since.

Ted sighed. "Everyone keeps trying to pair me

12

up with someone, but I'm really not interested right now."

"No one said you had to be involved with anyone right now. Come on, Ted. Cheer up. Look at me. I'm on my own.

"Hey, I just had a great idea! Why don't you come to Montana with me during Christmas vacation?" Bart said. "You'll love the ranch. I'll teach you to ride, and the mountains are incredible — there's no place in the world like it. We'll be two bachelors enjoying the outdoor life. It'll be great."

Ted looked surprised and a little interested. "That doesn't sound too bad. Do you think your parents would mind?"

"My mom suggested that Diana and I invite some friends from Rose Hill for Christmas. You know my mom, she loves having guests."

"I'll talk to my folks about it," Ted said, beginning to get excited. "I've heard so much about that ranch of yours. It would be nice to see it." They grinned at each other broadly as they strode into the building, laughing and talking about all the mischief they could get into in Montana.

What they saw when they walked through the door stopped them both. The hallway of the school was hardly recognizable. The walls, ceilings, and lockers — every available space — were covered with crepe-paper streamers, balloons, and signs. The building was bursting with festivity and excitement. GO KENNEDY! BEAT LEESBURG! and CARDINALS ARE THE BEST! stood out on large

13

banners that hung from the ceiling. Even though classes didn't start for fifteen minutes, it seemed like everyone was already there and the noise level in the hallway was deafening. Students' faces glowed with excitement and many of them wore "Beat Leesburg!" buttons.

"This is great!" Bart grinned at Ted over the din around them as they began walking to their lockers. "Go, Cardinals!" yelled someone passing them. Other students neither of them knew stopped to wish them luck in the game. By the time they got to Ted's locker, they both felt like celebrities.

"Hey, look at that!" Ted said excitedly, pointing to his locker door. It was covered with white paper, streamers, balloons, and a banner that said, TED MASON, KENNEDY HIGH'S STAR QUARTERBACK! GOOD LUCK AGAINST LEESBURG, TED!!

The boys looked at each other and laughed. "I can't believe how up everybody is for this game!" Ted said, shaking his head. "I'll bet the bleachers will be packed!"

Bart looked around at the decorations as he thanked several students who stopped to wish him luck in the game. "Why is everybody so excited about tonight?" he asked as Ted got his books and slammed his locker door. "I thought last week's game against Bradley was more important. They were rated higher than Leesburg — at least until we beat them."

"Because Leesburg is a military academy. Sports are a bigger deal in their school than ours. They're out to win no matter what, and sometimes they play dirty, like they did last year. That's why it was such a pleasure beating them last fall. Remember when I told you about pouring pink paint over a statue after one of the games? That was Leesburg's statue of General Robert E. Lee. They're still mad about it."

Bart chuckled. "So what's planned for them tonight?"

Ted shook his head. "Nothing. I hope. I don't want any part of that kind of thing anymore. We're just lucky we didn't get in trouble with the police last year. The coach benched me for one game and that was bad enough. It was a really stupid thing to do."

They stopped at Bart's locker, where they found another sign reading, BART EINERSON, KENNEDY HIGH'S STAR DEFENSIVE END! GOOD LUCK AGAINST LEESBURG, BART! Bart grinned, his handsome face full of pleasure. "I don't believe this," he said, shaking his head. "I feel famous." He took a mock bow and said, "I just hope my chauffeur doesn't forget to show up this afternoon."

"Want to go see Georgetown's football game tomorrow?" Ted asked, ignoring Bart's joke. "They play Roosevelt. It'll be a good match. Or maybe you'll be busy with Heather," he teased, punching him in the ribs.

"Hey, guys, all ready for tonight?" Phoebe Hall stopped at Bart's locker. Her green eyes were dancing with excitement.

"Sure, we're ready," Ted said warmly. He gave Phoebe's copper-colored braid a friendly tug. "You'll be there, of course?"

"Of *course! Nobody's* going to miss this game, Ted." Phoebe smiled. "I can't remember when I was looking forward to a football game so much. Can you guys come to the sub shop after the game? Everyone'll be there for the big celebration."

Bart and Ted nodded. "We'll be there," Bart said. "How about Michael, Phoebe? Is he coming to the game?"

"He's playing cello with a chamber group tonight, but he'll be there before it's over," Phoebe answered. "Have you guys registered for Student Council College Days yet? The lists of appointments with college recruiters are filling up fast. I'm on my way to sign up now." She sighed. "I wish I was as sure of what I wanted to do as Michael is."

"What about your singing?" asked Ted. "I always thought you were pretty serious about that."

"I am serious about it. I just don't know if there's a future in it for me. You have to be really great to make it professionally. Think they'd like me on Broadway?" She paused thoughtfully. "Have you heard anything about scholarships, Ted?"

Ted shook his head. "The coach thinks I've got a good chance at a couple. But it'll be a few months before I hear anything."

"What about you, Bart?"

He shrugged. "I'm not counting on a scholarship. I have a feeling I'll end up somewhere back West." He grinned at her. "Guess I'd better go visit some campuses and check out the girls be-

16

fore I fill out any applications."

She made a face at him. "That sounds like you, Bart. Obviously, we all know what your major is going to be. See you at lunch, guys."

"It's too bad she goes out with Michael Rifkin," Bart said.

"I don't think it would make a difference if she weren't. She goes for the artistic, brainy types," Ted said, watching Phoebe as she walked away. "Did you know she went out with Brad Davidson last year?"

"You mean Brenda's boyfriend, the one at Princeton?"

"Yep, that's the one," interjected Woody Webster, who was opening his locker, which was next to Bart's. Woody was wearing his red suspenders, as usual. He gave Bart and Ted a toothy grin, his thick eyebrows moving up and down expressively.

"You two jocks," Woody went on, "have nothing to offer girls but muscle. That's your problem. Of course, if you win against Leesburg tonight, you can name your own terms — every girl in school will be at your feet."

A loud ringing broke into their conversation. "First bell," Bart said. "I gotta get upstairs to my homeroom. See you at lunch, Ted. Later, Woody," he called, moving quickly down the hall.

As he passed Mr. Nelson's room, he stopped and stuck his head in the door, waving to Diana. She was engrossed in a conversation, but she saw him and waved back. Diana had made a quick, successful adjustment to the move from Montana and to a new school. She had been shy and home-

17

sick at first, but meeting Jeremy Stone had changed all that.

Bart liked Jeremy and he was happy for Diana, but he felt he was growing distant from her. Because their Montana ranch was kind of isolated, the two of them had spent a lot of time together. Now for the first time, though he'd hate to admit it, Bart felt like he needed Diana, and she was spending most of her time with Jeremy. He had become her confidant and best friend, and Bart was merely the older brother, ready to supply advice, but Diana didn't seem to realize that Bart also had some problems of his own.

But he did. On the outside he was brash, handsome Bart, a good student, popular, and one of the star football players. Inside, he was worried. He had to make some decisions about his future and he was concerned about his parents. He felt that the move to Washington had placed a strain on their relationship. Also, as much as he loved football and as confident as he was in his playing abilities, he was worried about the game against Leesburg. Diana could share her worries with Jeremy, but Bart didn't have anyone special. Ted was a good friend, but he wasn't sure Ted would understand.

Bart had had lots of girl friends, but never one special one. He'd always dated girls like Heather who —

"Bart! Hi!"

He looked up to see Heather coming toward him. He gave her a confident smile as she approached, her bright blonde curls bouncing behind her, one of her friends at her side.

18

"I can't believe I'm seeing you again today already," she said. "It must be fate."

"Just your good luck, Heather," Bart said teasingly, continuing down the hall to homeroom.

"And I'll see you tonight, too," Heather called after him.

Bart turned around and flashed his most devastating smile at her. As Heather watched, he quickly rounded the corner and was out of sight.

Chapter
3

Laurie Bennington caught up with Bart as he walked out of homeroom on his way to math. "Hi, Bart. Excited about your first game against Leesburg? I can hardly *wait* till tonight's game."

Bart started to reply but she interrupted him. "I'm going over to sign up for College Days. I want to talk to reps from all of the best Northeastern schools. What about you? Want to come sign up with me?"

He frowned and shook his head. "Not yet. I'll take care of it later."

"Where are you going to college?" Laurie asked as they edged into the flow of students in the hallway.

"I don't know yet. The University of Montana, maybe," Bart mumbled absently. He wasn't anxious to talk about college. His future felt too unsettled.

Laurie stopped, forcing the students behind her

to detour around her. "The University of Montana!" she said loudly, her hands on her hips.

As students stopped to stare, Bart signaled for Laurie to keep walking. She caught up to him again, shaking her head in amazement. "C'mon, Bart, you can do better than *that*. Why go to some hick university when you can go anywhere you want? Any prestigious Eastern college will take you. After all, Bart, your father *is* a *congressman*. If you go to graduate school, having attended an Ivy League school as an undergraduate will be a big advantage."

Bart decided against trying to defend himself. Laurie would never understand if he told her that what he wanted more than anything was to run the family ranch and that the University of Montana could prepare him for that occupation far better than any prestigious Eastern school.

He couldn't imagine himself anywhere else. He loved the horses, the cattle, and the cycles of the work day. Most of all he loved the land. What experience could possibly equal the thrill of riding into an endless sunset, or of settling in next to a blazing fire during a Montana blizzard? But he couldn't tell Laurie Bennington that.

"I simply can't decide if I want to be an anchorperson on TV or open a chain of jazzy boutiques," Laurie said. "I know so much about clothes, you know, but Daddy can get me started on TV at his cable network. Of course, he'd set me up in business, too, if I wanted." She sighed dramatically. "I just *can't* decide. I'll probably major in business *and* in communications and then I'll be ready for either."

Bart glanced at Laurie out of the corner of his eye. She always wore flashy clothes from exclusive Georgetown boutiques and was known for the expensive parties she threw. She was one of those people who never thought about people's feelings before she spoke.

"You didn't mean that, did you, Bart?"

"You mean about going to a hick college out West?" Bart grinned at her. "Naw, I was just joking. I'll probably try for one of the Ivy League schools here in the East."

"You really should," Laurie said in a business-like manner. "Where you go is very important for your career."

"You're right," Bart nodded. He didn't feel like arguing with her. Why try to explain himself to one more person who obviously couldn't understand why the ranch was so important to him? Laurie Bennington could think whatever she wanted. It wouldn't change how he felt.

Kristi Marshall made a point of sitting next to Bart in math, batting her big blue eyes at him whenever she had a chance. Without even thinking about it, Bart returned her flirtatious overtures, frequently flashing her a broad grin and acting like he was interested in her. But after class he left quickly, knowing she expected him to talk to her. He didn't know why it was so hard for him to keep from flirting. He had no interest in the girls that threw themselves at him, but somehow he couldn't get himself to act any other way.

His favorite class was next, economics small

group with Ms. Tyler. She always led interesting discussions and he really felt like he was learning things that mattered in her class. All of the juniors and seniors taking economics met twice a week in the auditorium for lectures by one of the three teachers who taught the course, and met three times a week for small group discussions with twelve to fifteen students.

Bart knew he was lucky to have Ms. Tyler as his econ small group teacher. Right now she was working on arrangements for her students to interview economists in the federal government — something the other teachers weren't doing. The class would travel by school bus to Capitol Hill in Washington to conduct the interviews.

The fifteen chairs in Ms. Tyler's classroom were arranged in a circle and most of them were already filled when Bart walked in. He sat down next to Gene Watkins, a second-string offensive tackle on the football team, and they began to talk about the game.

When Ms. Tyler came in, the class grew quiet. She quickly took the roll, then looked around the group. "We have a new student joining us today," she announced. "A junior named Holly Daniels. She's transferring in from Mr. Hoover's section, but I see she isn't here yet."

Hearing a knock, she turned toward the door. A moment later Holly stepped in, obviously embarrassed at being late.

"You must be Holly," Ms. Tyler said warmly. "We were expecting you. Come join us."

Holly quickly sat down in the only vacant chair in the circle and immediately opened her notebook. She was sitting directly across from Bart.

He watched her, then realized he was staring at her. She was so pretty it almost took his breath away. Holly Daniels. Her name fit her perfectly —she looked pure and fresh.

When he could finally take his eyes off her face, he noticed how the color of her sweater — a soft aqua-blue — set off her curly brown hair and green eyes. Or were they brown? He couldn't tell for certain from across the circle. She was small, almost petite, and very slender.

He couldn't believe he had never seen her before. How could he have been in the same building with her for the past six weeks without noticing her? But then, it was a big school, and the people he knew were either part of his crowd, in his classes, or on the football team. The other girls he knew were ones who let him know they were there — like Heather and Kristi Marshall — the ones who obviously wanted something from him. This girl, he could tell immediately, wasn't anything like that.

Holly glanced up at him, but when he smiled at her, she lowered her eyes. He wanted her to look at him again. He willed her to, but she kept her eyes on her notebook. He wanted to see her eyes, her face. He wanted her to smile at him, to notice him.

"Holly has qualified for the work release program," Ms. Tyler was saying. "She's changed small groups because on Tuesday and Thursday afternoons she works at the medical clinic at

Rose Hill Hospital. We're glad to have you with us, Holly.

Holly smiled at her. "Thank you."

Bart sat in wonder. Holly had a low, husky voice and when she smiled, her whole face lit up. She must be pretty smart, too — or she wouldn't be allowed to leave school to work two afternoons a week.

"We're going to continue our discussion of government financing today," Ms. Tyler continued, breaking into Bart's thoughts. "We were talking about U.S. Treasury Bonds. What is the face value of a government bond?" She looked around the circle. "Bart?"

He nervously cleared his throat, his pulse racing. "It's always a thousand dollars," he said carefully, his voice strained, "but the market value can be more or less. It depends on whether current interest rates are lower or higher than the day the bond was issued."

"Excellent, Bart," Ms. Tyler nodded. "You've done your homework. Now, can someone else tell me how often the fixed return on the bonds is paid and how bonds can be purchased?"

Bart knew that Holly had looked at him when he had answered the question. He felt just like he did when a big football play was coming up — excited, ready to meet the challenge, but scared to death that with a false move he could ruin everything.

The discussion continued, with Ms. Tyler carefully explaining in simple language the complexities of treasury bonds. Bart tried not to look at

Holly, who was taking rapid notes, but he found it impossible.

"Bart," he heard Ms. Tyler say, "if a bond is selling for less than its face value, why is that attractive to a potential buyer?"

He panicked for a moment. He hadn't been listening. He repeated her question, giving himself time to think. It was the first time he could remember having so much trouble concentrating in his favorite class. He answered the question perfectly, though, then daydreamed about Holly through the rest of the class. He kept thinking up different ways to approach her, unable to decide what would work best. He didn't remember ever feeling so self-conscious or nervous just because of a girl before.

"Jeez, Einerson, you trying to make the rest of us look like idiots or something?" Gene Watkins muttered to him when the class bell rang. "You gotta quit studying so hard, man. We can't keep up with you."

Bart laughed, hurriedly putting his papers away and picking up his books. "Sorry, pal. Bad habit of mine. I'll see you in the locker room tonight. I gotta rush right now — there's someone I want to talk to."

But when he looked around, Holly was gone.

Chapter
4

Holly walked rapidly away from Ms. Tyler's classroom, slowing down only after she had turned the corner and was on her way down the long hallway toward the library.

She didn't feel like eating the lunch she had packed. She would find a qiuet place at a secluded library table, open a book, and have some time to collect her thoughts before starting her afternoon classes.

She stepped around an effigy of a Leesburg football player hanging from the ceiling with a sign on it saying LEESBURG WILL HANG IN DEFEAT TONIGHT! Crepe paper streamers, signs, and balloons were everywhere. The whole school was so up for this game. What a bummer that she had to miss it.

The morning had gone well so far. She thought she had done well on the math quiz — afterward, when she and Diana had compared answers, they had seemed to come up with the same ones.

It looked like economics would be all right. Ms. Tyler seemed to be a good teacher — just like she'd heard. Econ was not one of her favorite subjects. She had decided to take it only because she knew it would be a good basic course to have — and it surprised her that the discussion on something as boring as treasury bonds had actually been sort of interesting, even though she got off to a bad start by being late. If she hadn't talked to Diana after class about the math quiz, she would have been on time.

She smiled as she remembered Bart and a shiver ran up her spine. He was gorgeous. He had smiled at her, but she didn't know if he was being friendly because he knew she was a friend of his sister's, or if he was flirting.

Diana had joked about how her brother flirted with everyone, so that must have been it. Holly frowned. Too bad. She knew the type — a typical, conceited football player who thought that every girl who said hello to him wanted to go out with him.

But then Holly remembered Bart had made some intelligent comments in class, so maybe it wasn't all true.

As she opened the library door, she heard someone behind her call her name. She turned around, astonished to see Bart hurrying toward her.

"Hi! You're not spending lunch in the library, are you?"

She felt herself blush and then was immediately annoyed at herself for letting him have such an

28

effect on her. Remember what he's like, she told herself. Just because he's *so* good-looking, with blue eyes, dark hair, and a square jaw, doesn't mean you have to become tongue-tied in front of him. She tried to collect her thoughts. How had he found her here? "I — wasn't going to eat today. I thought I'd go to the library and study instead," she said self-consciously. Her throat had gone dry.

"But it's a beautiful day," he protested, "and even if you don't eat, you need a break before the afternoon starts." Before Holly could refuse, Bart took her elbow and steered her back down the hall toward the wide doors that led to the outdoor quad.

"Your eyes," he said, looking at her intently, "they're hazel, aren't they? Depending on the light, they look either green or brown, but up close they're a combination." He grinned. "I was trying to decide in class."

"I — I know your sister," Holly stammered, changing the subject, in spite of being flattered by his interest in her eyes.

"Diana? How do you know her?"

"We're in the same math class. In fact, I called her before school this morning."

"I remember she was talking about an assignment with someone. Was that you?" He looked pleased. "How come I haven't seen you around school before?"

"I'm new this year."

"Me, too. Coming into a new school so late is a pain, isn't it? But so far Kennedy seems okay."

Holly smiled. "Yeah. I think so, too. You seem to like econ a lot, and you're good at it."

"It's my favorite subject," Bart said. "Catch me in some of my other subjects and it's a different story."

"Bart! Wait up!"

They turned to see Heather Richardson, two girl friends in tow, running toward them.

Holly knew Heather slightly. They had American history together. Heather was exactly the kind of girl that made Holly uncomfortable — with her flashy, revealing clothes and fancy car.

Heather never glanced at Holly. "Oh, Bart," she said breathlessly, sliding up close to him, "I just knew I'd find you in time for lunch. Going out to the quad? Don't tell anybody, but there's going to be a surprise pep rally out there in a few minutes."

Bart grinned at her. "Hey, great!" he said enthusiastically. "Pep band, too?"

"Of course!" Heather giggled. "So, I'll see you out there." She finally looked toward Holly and frowned. Holly started to smile, but stopped when Heather arched an eyebrow and gave her an up-and-down look obviously meant to make her squirm. "Bye," Heather said sweetly to Bart.

"See you later, Heather," he answered, opening the door for Holly.

As they walked onto the quad, she kept her eyes on the concrete. He had certainly confirmed her suspicions about him — just another jock who talked to all the pretty girls. He definitely wasn't her type. Steven, at the clinic, who was more mature, was the type she liked. He didn't have to flirt with every girl he encountered. She needed to find some excuse to leave so she could get away from Bart. She wasn't sure he was someone she was interested in getting to know, but there seemed to be no way out of having lunch with him now.

"I'd like to know more about your part-time job," Bart said, motioning to Holly to sit beside him on one of the wooden benches. "It must be really interesting working in an emergency room."

She reluctantly sat down, waiting for an opportunity to flee. "It's not just an emergency room," she said self-consciously, her voice sounding more husky and low-pitched than usual. "We're like a walk-in doctor's office, too. No appointment necessary." She kept her eyes on a group of students nearby who had taken their lunches out of their backpacks and were sitting on the concrete, soaking up the noonday sun. Bart seemed to be waiting for her to say something else. She tried to think. "Lots of people drop in just because they see the clinic and suddenly remember that they want to check with a doctor about something. We're quick, and we're always open."

"How did you get the job?" he asked curiously.

Holly glanced at him. He was ignoring everything going on around him, his attention completely focused on her. His piercing gaze made her shiver, and she tried to concentrate carefully on her words. "I saw an ad for the job and I talked the physician who runs the clinic into giving me a chance," she explained. "I told him I was thinking about a career in nursing and if I didn't get some experience, I'd never find out if

31

it was right for me or not." She laughed, remembering her first discussion with Dr. Ellerbee. Feeling a little more comfortable with Bart, she told him how she had gotten herself so worked up for the interview that she hadn't given the doctor any way to turn her down.

"I'd like to see the clinic sometime," Bart said. "There's nothing like it where I come from, and it sounds like the kind of place a rural town could use. There's a real shortage of doctors in Montana."

"You'd enjoy talking to Dr. E.," Holly said, warming up to him. Bart was becoming surprisingly easy to talk to. There seemed to be two very different sides to him. He asked intelligent questions and seemed genuinely interested in what she was doing. "He's a well-known doctor around here. Lots of specialists refer their patients to him."

She met Bart's eyes and smiled at him, laughing self-consciously.

"I thought I recognized that laugh! Hi, Holly." Phoebe Hall, her copper-colored braid bobbing behind her, dropped her books and hugged Holly, then plopped to the ground, her eyes twinkling. "It's so great that you're back in Rose Hill! I keep hoping we'll run into each other for more than a few minutes and really have a chance to catch up."

"Me, too, Phoebe," Holly said shyly. "How's your family?"

"My parents are great and little brother Shawn's a royal pain, as usual. Nothing's

32

changed," Phoebe laughed. "So how's your mom doing?" she asked eagerly.

"Fine. She's dating a guy named Bruce. It looks serious," Holly answered.

"You like him?"

"He's okay. Mom's happy, so I'm happy."

"I take it your parents are divorced," Bart broke in. A shadow crossed his face. "That must be rough."

"I'm used to it. I don't mind anymore," Holly said matter-of-factly.

"Holly and I used to live practically next door to each other," Phoebe explained to him. "We were best friends for a long time. Boy, did I miss you after you moved away." She grinned at Holly.

"Hey, Einerson! How come you let Owens and Gibbs get through you on the line last night at practice? Don't you know anything?" John Marquette was suddenly there in front of them. Marquette's criticism apparently hit a sensitive spot, judging from the look on Bart's face. Even though Holly was new at Kennedy, she knew Marquette's reputation as a bully who threw his weight around and used enough unsportsmanlike conduct to keep Coach Briggs, the Kennedy High football coach, perpetually nervous.

Phoebe glared at John. "Leave us alone, Marquette. Since when are you Mr. Perfect?" she challenged.

Marquette looked at her and then back at Bart. "You let girls talk for you, Einerson?" he sneered.

"Cool off, Marquette," Bart said in an irritated voice. "You know we're going to win tonight. And don't worry — I learn from my mistakes. Nobody's getting through the line tonight."

"They better not," Marquette said gruffly. "We're gonna give Leesburg a defeat to remember. I'll make sure of that! And after we beat them we're gonna have some fun," he added, winking at Bart. "Wanna join us, Einerson? We have some plans for dressing up their hot-shot campus."

"No thanks," Bart said disapprovingly. "I prefer to settle my scores on the football field."

"Yeah? I'd say it looks like you'll be otherwise occupied after the game, too," Marquette taunted, giving Holly an openly appraising gaze.

Bart shifted uncomfortably. "That's right, Marquette, there are things I'd rather do with my time," Bart said, looking at Holly and feeling sheepish, but wanting to get rid of Marquette.

Holly froze, embarrassed. She hardly knew Bart! How could he say such a thing?

Marquette leered at her, making her blush. "Well, maybe by the end of the game you'll change your mind."

The quad was getting crowded and Marquette moved away, pushing his way into a small group of football players who were congregating nearby.

"John Marquette will never change," Phoebe said, disgusted.

Bart glanced at Holly. "Sorry if I embarrassed you. I didn't know how to get rid of the guy."

"No problem," Holly said stiffly, annoyed at the way Bart had used her.

"Somebody ought to stop him before he does something stupid tonight," Phoebe said. "He could make a fool of himself *and* Kennedy High. Everyone still talks about last year when Ted Mason — "

"Someone taking my name in vain?" Ted walked up behind Phoebe. She turned in surprise and laughed. Jeremy Stone and Diana Einerson, holding hands, also joined them. Diana looked pleased to see Holly and gave her a warm smile. She sat down next to her and introduced her to Jeremy.

"Looks like you've met my ugly brother," Diana said, reaching around Holly to give Bart a friendly poke.

"We're in the same econ small group now. Do you take econ, Phoebe?" Holly asked, glancing down at her old friend.

Phoebe wrinkled her nose. "I took it last year. From Mr. Roseman. What a drag! Remind me not to take it in college next year."

"Pheeberooni! How's the world treating you?" Woody Webster plopped down on the ground next to Phoebe and threw an arm around her, giving her a squeeze. Kim Barrie, his girl friend, sat down beside him.

"Hi, everybody," she grinned. Her eyes stopped on Holly. "Hello, I'm Kim Barrie," she said politely.

Holly introduced herself.

"Holly and I are friends from way back," Phoebe told Kim. "We went to grade school together. She's just moved back to Rose Hill from Baltimore."

35

Phoebe's eyes met Holly's and both girls smiled.

Chris Austin and her stepsister Brenda were making their way across the quad toward the crowd. Diana and Phoebe introduced them to Holly and they both smiled at her. Holly couldn't believe how friendly everyone was. She felt so comfortable with all of them as they sat around joking and talking about school activities. Bart and Diana were kidding each other, first leaning in front of Holly, then in back of her, with good-natured barbs that had everyone, including Holly, laughing.

Sasha Jenkins, her long, dark brown hair swirling around her shoulders, approached Phoebe and Kim. Holly knew that Sasha was the editor of the school paper. She was with Janie Barstow. Holly had heard about the successful business Janie had started with her boyfriend, Henry Braverman, a dress designer.

Sasha, Phoebe, and Kim looked at each other, and then clapped their hands to get the gang's attention. "We have an announcement to make," Kim said.

"It's about a party," Phoebe said.

"A very *special* party," Sasha added.

"A week from Saturday night, a Halloween costume party, at the Albatross — the Jenkinses' bookstore," Kim said.

"Come as your favorite character from literature," Sasha said.

"Prizes for the best costumes," Kim interjected.

"And food catered by Earthly Delights,"

Phoebe added, referring to the catering service Kim's mother ran, famous for its delicious sweets.

Everyone began to chatter excitedly, talking about the party and possible costumes. Then Jeremy stood up on a bench. "I have an announcement, too," he said, clearing his throat. Everybody turned to look at him. "Most of you know I have a younger sister named Fiona. When my father was appointed to the staff of the British Embassy in Washington, I wanted to come along, but my sister stayed in England to continue her ballet studies," he said in his cultured British accent. "Well, now Fiona is taking a leave from her studies and is coming for a long visit. In fact," Jeremy added, smiling, "she may decide to stay permanently — *if* she gets on well with the faculty at the Academy of Ballet Arts in Georgetown, and *if* she likes Rose Hill."

Diana stood up next to Jeremy. "So we need everyone to help Fiona feel at home, because if she likes it here, she'll stay."

"She's arriving over the weekend, and I hope to get her to visit Kennedy High one day next week," Jeremy added.

"Why don't you bring her to our party?" Sasha suggested.

"Of course! It'll be a great way for everyone to get to know her," Phoebe agreed.

They all began to talk about how to make Fiona like Rose Hill, Kennedy High, and living in the United States. Holly was touched by the conversation. She had always considered this crowd to be in their own privileged world — no one really taking the time to think about anyone not in their group — but here they were, going out of their way to think of ways to make someone new feel at home.

They were doing the same thing for her — going out of their way to be friendly. Already she felt like a part of their crowd. Phoebe had already told her that of course she was included in the party invitation and that she would be very disappointed if Holly didn't come.

"I might have to work," Holly warned her, "otherwise, I'd love to come. Thanks for the invite, Phoebe."

Phoebe's eyes were shining. "I'm just so glad we've rediscovered each other," she said softly. "We've got lots of times to talk over." She glanced at Bart. "So what do you think of our Montana cowboy?"

Holly blushed. "Well, he's very cute, but I don't think he's my type," she whispered back, strongly aware of Bart's physical presence and the undeniable attraction she felt for him.

"He might surprise you," Phoebe whispered thoughtfully. "Sometimes you just have to give someone a chance. That was true for Michael and me."

"Michael?"

"My boyfriend," Phoebe smiled happily. "Michael Rifkin. He's a musician. You'll meet him soon."

"Is this a private conversation, or can I cut in?" Sasha asked, squatting down next to Phoebe. She smiled at Holly. "I hope you'll be able to come to the party," she said.

"I'll try. I've been in your parents' bookstore

and I love it. It's a great place for a party."

"It's going to be a little tight on dancing space, but otherwise it should be perfect. We're going to push most of the bookcases to the sides to make room. And we'll use the cash register area for the food. I'm trying to be optimistic about everything," she laughed. "Guess what, Pheeb, I got a letter from Rob yesterday and he says he'll be able to come! He has to work Saturday but he'll leave right after work, so he should get here just in time."

"Sasha's boyfriend goes to college at St. John's in Annapolis," Phoebe explained to Holly. "It's a long-distance romance. I'm convinced that it's only working because Sasha wants to be a writer and she gets lots of practice writing letters to Rob."

"Very funny, Pheeb," Sasha said as she offered each of them a granola bar from her lunch. "I'm famous for these."

Holly reluctantly took one and bit into it. "Wow! This is delicious — "

Peter Lacey's voice interrupted her over the loudspeaker as he started his noontime show on WKND, the school radio station. "Listen up, Cardinal fans, it's time for some rock to munch lunch by," he said in his inimitable DJ style, the deep resonance of a bass guitar twanging behind him. "Here's the latest from a new Motown group who call themselves Gold Medallion."

Just as the music started, the pep band came bursting through one of the doors onto the quad, playing the school fight song. The pep squad, Heather prominently in the front, followed behind it. Each of the girls carried pom-poms and shook them in rhythm to the music. Everyone stood up, singing the song at the top of their voices, completely drowning out Peter's show.

The members of the squad began rounding up the football players on the quad, ushering them to the center where everyone could see them. Giggling, Heather came bouncing over and grabbed Bart's hand.

Holly felt a sharp pang of jealousy. She watched as Heather stood directly in front of Bart, her body bobbing up and down to the music of the fight song. Bart was grinning at her.

Holly was disappointed. Just when she'd thought he was different from her first impression of him, he let her down. He was just an immature high school jock ogling a pom-pom girl. But her jealousy surprised her. Why should she care how Heather acted toward Bart? She wasn't interested in him.

At the end of the song Heather threw her arms around Bart and gave him a hug. Holly couldn't tell for sure, but it looked like Bart was hugging her back.

Before the cheering ended, she slipped away, disappearing into the building.

Chapter 5

Bart sat at the breakfast bar in the Einerson kitchen, idly strumming his guitar and eyeing the hamburger in front of him. Usually he was ravenous before a game and could eat everything in sight. But tonight nothing tasted very good. If his mother had been here, he'd have had to force it down or she would worry that something was wrong.

He was the one who was worried, but not about being sick. He had walked in after school to find his mother on the telephone with his father, arguing about this evening, insisting that they should miss the State Department reception in order to see Bart's game. When she hung up, she was upset, explaining that if there was any way out of going to the reception so they could come to the game they would take it, but they simply had to be there.

It was a formal affair — something she hated

—— but she had dutifully bought an evening gown for it, and when she had left a few minutes earlier, taking a cab to meet Bart's dad at his office, she looked beautiful. Very *unlike* the ranch wife in jeans and a flannel shirt he was used to.

But she didn't look happy, and that was the problem. Bart knew she hated to miss the football game. Both of his parents always came if possible. He tried to assure his mother that he didn't mind, though secretly he minded very much. He told her Diana and the crowd would be there, and they would cheer him on. He also promised to get in early tonight to tell them all about the game.

"I wish that I had nothing to worry about but winning a football game," she sighed, and Bart had resisted the urge to tell her his problems. Instead he played the strong, fun-loving son she wanted and expected him to be.

He strummed his guitar again, smiling to himself. Even though he had a lot on his mind, one very nice thing had happened that day. He had met Holly. She hadn't been out of his mind much since.

But what had happened at lunch? One minute she was there, and the next minute she wasn't. He had watched for her all afternoon, but finding her would have been sheer luck. He'd have to start doing what Heather was doing to him —— stalking her.

On the other hand, Heather was *everywhere*! He had seen her twice that afternoon. He had never known a girl to be so obvious about her interest in him.

He took a tentative bite of the hamburger and then laid it down. Ugh! Tonight he would play on an empty stomach. Maybe he would be hungry after the game when everybody met at the sub shop.

Diana came strolling into the kitchen and sat down at the breakfast bar facing him. She picked out an apple from the fruit bowl and began to polish it. "Hi ya, big guy, ready for the game?"

He smiled slightly. "Sure. I'm always ready to play football."

Diana gave him a quizzical look, her eyes dropping to his uneaten hamburger and then back to his face. She started to say something, then stopped. She gave him a gentle punch in the shoulder. "So how did Mom look when she left? Did you like the dress I helped her pick out?"

"What?" Bart looked distracted. "Oh, the dress. Yeah. I thought it was great. She looked terrific. Dad should flip when he sees her."

Diana's expression softened. "That would be nice, wouldn't it? Maybe they'll have a wonderful, romantic evening."

"At a State Department reception? Don't count on it," Bart said sarcastically. "Mom didn't want to go and she'll probably make sure she has a rotten time."

"Don't be that way, Bart. Everything's going to work out. You'll see."

He stared hard at her. "You've got your head in the clouds, Di. Mom's not happy here."

"Don't say that!" Diana said sharply. "If you and I are happy here, then she'll be happy, and she and Dad will try to work things out."

"That's crazy."

"No it isn't. Mom told me that more than anything she wants us to be happy. If *we* are, then she is. And if she is, then Dad is. And if they're both happy, then she'll probably start to like Washington."

Bart looked doubtful. "You really think it's that simple?"

"Yes, I really do. So are we going to win tonight?"

Bart gave her a confident grin, trying to hide his troubles. "With me playing? Of course."

"If you were back home, you'd be the quarterback tonight," Diana reminded him. "Does it bother you that Ted beat you out for it here?"

Bart shrugged. "He was better than me. I'm probably lucky I even made the team since I came in as a senior transfer."

She looked at his hamburger again. "Why aren't you eating? Your huge appetite before a game is legendary. Something wrong?"

"Just not hungry. Nothing's wrong."

"Aren't you excited about the costume party?" she asked, changing the subject. "Jeremy and I are going as Tweedledee and Tweedledum. Doesn't that sound like a riot? We'll find huge clothes and stuff them with pillows and get identical beanies and put freckles all over our faces."

Bart smiled approvingly. "Sounds great. I remember when Mom read us *Through the Looking Glass*. We used to play-act all the characters."

"We looked at the book today and it just seemed like a natural choice to us. Jeremy's always liked the book, too. What are you going as?"

"Adam Smith's *Wealth of Nations*," he said with a grin.

"Stop talking economics," she said with mock disgust. "That's not literature. What's your favorite *literary* book?"

Bart shrugged. "I've never been much of an English student."

"But you like to read — what novel do you remember as a favorite?"

"*Shane.*"

"That would be great!" Diana said enthusiastically. "You could dress in fringed buckskin with a wide leather belt and — "

"And wear silver spurs and a white Stetson," finished Bart, suddenly excited. "Hey, I like that idea. I've got everything but the shirt, and I bet I could find that in a Western shop or a costume store."

"Well, it will certainly be true to character for you. You make a great cowboy."

Bart smiled. "Think so? Then that settles it — I'll go as Shane."

Diana stuck out her tongue at him. "None of us missed the play Heather made for you this afternoon at the pep rally. Anything going on with her?"

"I never saw her before today."

"Well, she's your type," Diana sighed. "You've dated a million girls just like her."

Bart stared hard at his sister. "Why do you say that?"

"C'mon, Bart, they're all alike."

"Maybe my type is changing," Bart said thoughtfully. He smiled. "I could be interested in your friend Holly, for example."

"Ha! Good luck, Bart, but I don't think you stand a chance."

He looked at her in surprise. "Why not?"

"I don't know her real well yet, but Holly's very level-headed and serious. Somehow I just can't see you two together."

"Well, I can be serious and level-headed," Bart retorted. "I'm a good student and I — "

"Besides, she's interested in someone else."

"Oh!" Bart felt like he'd been punched in the stomach. He wasn't used to competition when it came to girls. "Who is he?"

"I don't know his name. She told me about him last week. He's a pre-med student who works at the clinic where she has her part-time job."

Bart tried to keep his voice nonchalant. "Well, I guess I figured it was worth a try."

"Hey, don't look so dejected. The game starts in two hours and you're going to be a standout. It'll be your best game ever. I'll be there screaming my lungs out!"

"Thanks, Di." Bart gave her a determined grin and took a big bite of his hamburger. He raised his glass of milk to her in a toast. "To my best game ever. Beat Leesburg!"

Chapter
6

"Diana! Over here!"

Kim stood up in her stadium seat and waved to Diana, who was climbing up the steps to the spot where the crowd always sat to watch football games. She had just left Jeremy at the sidelines so he could take pictures of the game for the school newspaper.

Diana saw them and waved back as she worked her way over to where the whole gang was seated. Everyone was wearing the school colors and spirits were running high. The stadium was packed with a capacity crowd. The weather was football-perfect — a clear, crisp fall evening.

Diana squeezed in between Phoebe and Sasha. Janie and Brenda were in front of them and the rest of the group was behind them.

Diana felt exhilarated. Here she was, surrounded by her friends, with her brother and his teammates about to enter the field for the biggest game of the year. She just wished Jeremy could be here in the stands with her, but he was so excited at the prospect of taking pictures for the paper that she was happy for him.

The pep squad was warming up in front of the crowd, leading everyone in school cheers. Groups in the stadium were starting cheers on their own, and the crowd's spirit was building. Across the field, the visitors' area was jammed with Leesburg fans. They had male yell leaders who returned every chant started by the Kennedy pep squad with their own. The crowd rivalry was vocal and heated by the time the two teams came running onto the field to the thunderous applause of their cheering sections.

The yelling and cheering increased as the players lined up and were introduced by the announcer over the loudspeaker. Next to her, Diana felt Sasha give a start when the announcer introduced Leesburg's star running back, Wesley Lewis. She knew Sasha had dated Wes for a while last year.

The Kennedy crowd roared its approval when quarterback Ted Mason was introduced. They cheered just as loudly when Bart's name was announced. Diana was on her feet, yelling and clapping as loudly as she could in support of her brother. She couldn't help notice that one member of the pep squad was cheering even louder than the others. Heather Richardson was making a real spectacle of herself. When Bart stepped forward as his name was announced, she bounced around, screaming her lungs out.

Diana wasn't the only one who noticed. "Looks like Bart has his own fan club," Woody commented, pointing to Heather.

Diana had never understood football very well, but even she could tell as the game started that the two teams were well matched. Neither one made much progress against the other, and the crowds settled in for what had all the appearances of being a long, grueling game.

"Bart's off to a super start," Woody said behind her. "Did you see that tackle he just got? I could tell today at school that he was really revved up for tonight. Leesburg better watch out for him!"

When Wesley Lewis was replaced by another Leesburg player, Phoebe put a sympathetic arm around Sasha. "Is it sort of tough watching him down there?" she asked in a kind voice.

Sasha shrugged, keeping her brown eyes straight ahead. "It's — well, not tough, but I will admit that seeing him makes me think about him, and then lots of memories come back." She sighed. "Do you know that just a year ago I thought that the only thing I wanted in the world was to spend the rest of my life with him? Things can really change fast."

Suddenly the crowd let out a thunderous cheer and everyone around them rose to their feet. Phoebe turned to Woody and shouted over the roar, "What happened?"

He looked at her with mock disgust, his hands on his hips. "You just missed one of the best plays ever! Ted got a touchdown, that's what!"

The girls began to whoop and cheer. With the first quarter almost over, Kennedy was leading 6-0. The Kennedy fans were in an uproar. Then, within minutes, Leesburg not only got control of the ball, but also scored a touchdown and the extra point, pulling ahead 7-6. The game was heating up.

Diana tried to concentrate on what was happening. She could see Jeremy down on the sidelines, running along with the teams and snapping pictures, and she was far more interested in watching him than in what the teams were doing. With every play, the fans jumped to their feet and blocked her view.

She had almost given up trying to follow the action, when Brenda leaped to her feet. "I don't believe it! Marquette actually jumped on that player!" she shouted. Diana stood up along with everyone else. Down on the field she could see some sort of pile-up of players from both teams. Coach Briggs had come onto the field and had pulled Marquette aside. One referee was talking to the coach and another one was pulling players off the pile.

"What's going on? Are those guys fighting — or trying to stop a fight?" someone asked. The announcer was also confused. "We have an unusual situation on the field, folks," he said over the loudspeaker. "Whatever happened, it looks like everything will be back to normal in a minute. The players are all getting up now — but wait!"

Everyone strained to see what was happening on the field. Diana jumped up and down trying to

50

get a glimpse over the crowd in front of her. She saw Heather with her hands over her mouth while another member of the pep squad stood next to her patting her back. Then she saw that all of the players in the pile-up had gotten up and were standing around a figure who lay on the ground in obvious pain.

Diana heard herself cry out, and from behind she felt Kim's comforting touch.

The player still lying on the ground was Bart.

Chapter 7

"I've got to go down there!" Diana cried, one hand over her mouth, her eyes filling with tears. "He really looks like he's in pain. I've got to go down there."

"Let's wait a minute," Phoebe said soothingly, one arm comfortingly around Diana's shoulder. "Let's see if he gets up."

The announcer came over the loudspeaker. "It's Bart Einerson who's down, ladies and gentlemen. It's still not clear what happened, but apparently some kind of ruckus started on the field and Einerson got caught in the middle of it. They're bringing a stretcher onto the field for him now. Looks like he's out of the game."

Diana watched, horrified, her eyes glued to the field below them as her brother was carefully placed on the stretcher and carried off the field. Bart had never been injured in a game before — he was one of those people who was always cautious about safety. He never drove recklessly, drank, or took unnecessary chances. He had played football the same way, warming up thoroughly before each game and learning how to anticipate a blow from an opposing player so he wouldn't get hurt. Somehow he had been caught off guard, something very out of character for him.

The Kennedy fans clapped for Bart as he was carried from the field. Immediately they cheered his replacement and the second quarter was underway.

Around her, Diana's friends expressed their concern to each other and to her. "I think he was hit from behind," Woody said, his deep voice rising over the others. "The way he was lying on the field was awkward. Something wasn't quite right about it."

Diana felt tears streaming down her cheeks. "I've got to go down there," she said again. "Mom and Dad aren't here tonight. I've got to find out if he's okay and let them know."

"Woody and I will go with you," Kim said. "He knows how to get down to the locker room and they might let him go in. Let's go."

Diana smiled gratefully at them through her tears. "Thanks, guys. I really appreciate it."

"Good luck," Phoebe said, her voice full of concern.

Sasha patted Diana on the back as she was getting up. "He'll be okay. Maybe he just got the wind knocked out of him," she said hopefully.

Diana nodded, biting her lip. "Maybe," she said, trying to smile. "Maybe he was just tired and wanted to rest a few minutes," she tried to joke. Her eyes filled up with tears again as she and Kim and Woody worked their way to the aisle and moved quickly down the bleacher steps, avoiding the boys selling concessions, and dodging several small children running up the steps who were giggling and shouting to one another.

They stopped in the cemented tunnel-like area outside the locker room. "Ah, I do love a mystery," Woody said with a dramatic flourish, putting an ear to the door and pretending to listen.

"Woody, stop clowning around and go see what you can find out," Kim said. "Don't make Diana wait."

Woody nodded and opened the door, waving to Kim and Diana as he disappeared. Diana stared blankly at the closed door. What if Bart was seriously injured? What if he couldn't play football anymore? He loved football. And making the team at Kennedy had meant instant recognition by the student body, which was important to him. He had tried to fit in and to make friends — if anything, he had come on a little too strong, but things were evening out. Only . . . only now he was injured. . . .

"They'd have an ambulance here by now if the injury was really serious," Kim said, trying to offer comfort. "Maybe they're just going to have him sit out the rest of the game."

Diana nodded. "I know you're probably right, but you know how it is — when someone gets hurt, you automatically start thinking of all the awful things that could have happened until you find out what's wrong."

Kim stood close to her. They continued to wait in silence.

Woody finally returned, a frown on his face. "The team doctor is in there with him but I can't find out anything. They've got him in this little room and they wouldn't let me come in. Everybody seemed pretty calm. It must not be an emergency, because as far as I could tell, they haven't called an ambulance yet."

The three of them leaned against the cement wall of the tunnel, their eyes on the locker room door, waiting for it to open.

Suddenly they heard someone sniffling loudly and turned to see Heather and another pep squad member coming into the tunnel. "Really, Heather, he'll be okay," the girl was saying, patting Heather on the back. "Come back to the game. We need you for the cheers."

"I just *can't*," Heather wailed. "All I can think about is poor Bart. I've *got* to find out how he is. I just can't concentrate on anything else!"

She stopped when she saw Woody, Kim, and Diana. Recognizing Diana, she threw her arms around her. "Oh Diana, is he okay? What *happened* to him?"

"I — I don't know," Diana said, embarrassed by the way Heather was carrying on.

She looked helplessly at Woody and Kim, who rolled their eyes as Heather clung to Diana's neck.

"Those Leesburg players are going to pay for this. They were trying on purpose to get Bart out of the game because he's so good," Heather quivered.

"Uh, I don't think what happened really had

55

anything to do with Leesburg," Woody ventured. "It looked like our side started it, and Bart just got in the way."

Heather ignored him. "I just *know* his football career is over, and he was so *good*," she said sadly. Her girl friend drew her back from Diana's shoulder, much to Diana's relief, and tried to convince her to come back to the game. "You can come back and see him later," she was saying in soothing tones. "He'll be okay. Just come back to the game now."

Diana moved back a step, but Heather didn't seem to notice. "I have to go," she said dramatically. "The pep squad needs me. Promise me you'll come tell me as soon as you know how Bart is. And I want to see him. Just tell whoever's in charge that I'm on the pep squad." She looked earnestly into Diana's eyes. "Promise me."

Diana moved close to Woody, unsure what to say. "Look, I — "

"Thanks," Heather smiled, allowing her friend to pull her toward the exit. "I won't *breathe* until you come tell me."

"I won't *breathe* until you come tell me," Woody said, mimicking Heather after she left. "Jeez! She can be the star of our next drama production. That was quite a show. I've never even seen her with Bart."

"Are you going to tell him about her, Diana?" Kim asked.

"I don't know. All I can think about right now is how he is, and — "

"Out of the way, folks. Let us through."

Diana looked up, startled to see two ambulance

56

crew members coming into the tunnel. She and Woody and Kim flattened themselves against the wall and watched as the two men, one of whom carried a large medical bag, went into the locker room.

"At least they aren't blaring the ambulance siren," Woody said, "so it can't be too much of an emergency."

"Yeah, but it does mean they're taking him to a hospital," Kim said.

Diana's eyes filled with tears again. "I think I'd better go try to call my folks," she said, her voice quavering. "But I'm not sure how to get in touch with them." She tried to think. "Maybe the switchboard at my dad's office building can help me find them."

"Let's see if we can find out something about Bart first," Woody suggested. "The ambulance guys may be here just as a precaution." Kim put a comforting arm around Diana. "Want me to go find Jeremy?" she asked. "Maybe he should be here with you."

"That's okay," Diana said, trying to smile. "He's really busy with his photography. I don't want to take him away from that. Let's just see what happens, like Woody said."

The door of the locker room finally opened and the ambulance stretcher bed, with Bart lying on it, was rolled out. "Stay out of the way," cautioned one of the attendants, motioning to them. "Stay back."

Bart turned his head and saw them. He gave a faint smile, his face full of pain. "Hi, Diana," he said softly.

57

"Are you okay?" she asked in a small voice. "Why are they taking you to the hospital?"

"I'm — okay," he said, his face pale. "But I've hurt my shoulder. Gotta find out what I did, that's all. Sorry about all this."

Tears flowed down Diana's cheeks. "Don't be silly," she said. "The only thing that matters is how you are. Is it broken?" She motioned to his shoulder.

"Just loose," he said, closing his eyes in pain. "It just feels like it's come loose. I don't know how else to describe it."

They rolled the ambulance bed to the edge of the concrete and then carried it the last few steps to the ambulance. Several people stood around watching. The team doctor came out of the locker room and Woody stopped him.

"Any idea what's wrong?" he asked.

The doctor shook his head. "Can't be sure," he said. "Could be several things. We need to get him x-rayed and thoroughly checked out. I'm sending him to a fine doctor who will take good care of him."

"I'm his sister," Diana said unsteadily, stepping forward. "I think I should try to get in touch with our parents."

"Yes, I think you should. Tell them to meet him at the medical clinic at Rose Hill Hospital."

Chapter
8

Holly stood in front of the mirror in the small restroom at the clinic and ran a comb through her curly hair. She studied her face critically, then added a little lip gloss to what she already had on.

She smoothed the straight skirt of her crisp white uniform and adjusted the collar of her jacket. She knew the uniform made her look older, and she felt older when she wore it, too. She also acted differently when she put it on, as though it transformed her personality, made her instantly more mature and professional, ready to assume any responsibility.

She went back to the middle of the three emergency examining rooms and resumed her task of rolling pressure bandages and putting them in the storage cupboard. It had been an unusually slow Friday night at the clinic. Of course that could change in an instant — a car crash, a home fire, or a multitude of other possibilities could suddenly turn a quiet evening into havoc. That was one of the fascinations of emergency medicine: One minute nothing was happening, and the next you were plunged into life and death situations that might keep you busy for hours.

So far this evening Dr. Ellerbee had only seen a five-year-old girl who had fallen off the porch and injured her pride more than anything else, and had treated a minor burn suffered by a woman when a stove pan caught fire. Right now he was on the phone talking to a young mother whose baby had the flu. Steven Ewing was administering a routine chest X ray to a warehouse employee who had been injured several months ago in an accident and had to be checked periodically in order to collect his insurance benefits. Cheryl, the receptionist who handled all the administrative work and also took incoming calls, was talking to her sister on the phone, trying to decide which movie to see on Saturday night.

Holly turned on the radio that sat on a wall shelf, keeping the sound low. Maybe she would be able to catch the half-time score of the Kennedy-Leesburg game on the local news.

"Gotta go," she heard Cheryl say from the reception area. "There's a call on the other line. I'll check with you later."

Before Holly could tune in the station, she heard the wall buzzer, alerting the staff that an ambulance was on its way in. "What is it, Cheryl?" she heard Dr. Ellerbee ask.

"Sports injury, doc. A player in the Kennedy-

60

Leesburg game. Not an emergency, but they want him looked at, just in case. Should be here in about six minutes."

Dr. Ellerbee continued talking on the phone to the young mother. Steven Ewing came in and looked around the room. "Holly, make sure this area is ready for an exam, will you? We'll put the ambulance patient here."

She turned off the radio. "The room's ready. I haven't had much to do tonight, so I went ahead, just in case," she said.

"Good girl." He eyed her appreciatively. "You know, you look older when you put on your uniform. At least sixteen-and-a-half."

She made a face at him and he laughed. He was always teasing Holly about her age. At first she was sensitive about it, but Steven's teasing was good-natured and he was just as quick to call himself "the old man" as he was to refer to her as "the kid."

She liked him better all the time. It wasn't just his lean good looks and his Brooklyn accent. She liked his sense of humor and the skill with which he treated patients. But one thing about Steven bothered her: He assumed that everyone who lived in Rose Hill — with a few exceptions — was a rich snob.

He had told her that his father was dead and his mother worked at two jobs to support him and his sisters. He was putting himself through college with scholarships and his job and he studied hard to keep his grades up so he would qualify for a scholarship to medical school.

When he finished, he planned to set up his

61

practice back in Brooklyn. Working at the Rose Hill clinic was just a job to help him get experience and pay his expenses. He said he knew he would only be happy in the long run living with and working with people like himself. He had no use for people born, as he put it, "with cash stuffed in their pockets and a key to the family law firm hung around their necks."

The last time he and Holly had worked the same shift, they took their break at the same time and shared a Coke in the small kitchen at the clinic. He had expressed his view on the general population of Rose Hill, and Holly had tried to offer a defense, telling him that most Rose Hill residents might have some advantages, but underneath they were just like everyone else, with the same problems, hopes, and dreams. Steven had cut her off, refusing to listen.

In some ways he was right, of course. Some people were like that. But Holly had lived on both sides of the fence. When her parents were married, they had had plenty of money and lived in a beautiful home. Now, she and her mother were conscious of what everything cost. But Holly also knew that you couldn't judge people on the basis of money. Diana Einerson and Phoebe Hall were good examples. They could both have whatever they wanted, but you'd never know either of them came from well-to-do families.

Of course there were also girls like Laurie Bennington, who didn't hesitate to let anybody know she came from a wealthy family. If Steven ever met Laurie, he'd have plenty to say.

Even though she didn't agree with him about some things, Holly still hoped that Steven would ask her out. She knew he was busy with his studies and work, but she also suspected that he liked her, and *everybody* had to take some time out for fun now and then.

About an hour ago they had almost collided in the tiny galley kitchen when she went in to fix herself a cup of tea and he was getting a Coke out of the refrigerator. He gave her a funny look and for a moment she thought he was going to ask her out. But he hadn't, and she felt a twinge of disappointment.

Now Steven was standing over her watching her roll bandages. "I can show you a faster way to do that," he said, reaching over and taking the bandage from her. She started to protest and playfully jabbed him in the ribs. "Give me back my bandage. I'll do it *my* way, *Dr.* Ewing." Steven grabbed her hands and looked into her eyes and for an instant Holly thought he was going to kiss her.

"I was just thinking, Holly. Maybe we — " Steven paused and cocked his head.

Holly heard the siren, too, and a moment later the ambulance was pulling up in front of the clinic. Steven dropped her hand and ran outside to meet it.

She went into the reception area and stood beside Cheryl's desk. As the ambulance came to a stop, she felt her heart begin to race. What would it be this time? Every new situation in the clinic was a challenge to be met and conquered. Every patient needed the staff's skills and relied on them to see him through the crisis of the moment. Knowing how to interact with each person in order to get full cooperation from him was also important.

The ambulance attendants lifted the collapsible stretcher bed to the ground and rolled it into the clinic. Holly couldn't see the patient's face because one of the attendants was blocking it, but she immediately recognized the uniform. It was a Kennedy player! As she moved to the foot of the stretcher, she was startled to hear a familiar voice, a voice that was now very weak, say, "Holly. Hi."

Bart's blue eyes were open and looking at her. They were filled with pain.

"Bart!" she said, surprised. Even in a dirty football uniform, reeking of liniment, he was unbelievably attractive. And even in pain, the strong features of his face were appealing.

Steven looked from Bart to Holly and back again. "I take it you two know each other, right? Take him right in here, guys," he said, directing the ambulance attendants into the middle examining room. "Holly, help us get your friend's football jersey off. Looks like superjock got the worst of a hard tackle."

"It was a pile-up," Bart said weakly, trying to sit up and help. The movements made him grimace in pain, his face turning white. Holly began to cut the jersey off of him with a sturdy pair of scissors. She touched him as tenderly as she could, aware that Steven was watching her closely. So was Bart. She glanced at him and found him smil-

64

ing at her, and she knew she was blushing. "I feel better already," he said faintly.

But it was clear that he didn't. He sat on the edge of the table, gripping it tightly with his hands as they removed his football pads and Steven began to check his left shoulder. "Dr. Ellerbee will come in to examine you in a minute," Steven said in his most professional manner. "We're going to x-ray your shoulder, and I'm just checking how to see what angles we're going to want to shoot. Is the most intense pain back here, or under here?" he asked, applying light pressure to different areas of Bart's skin.

Holly watched as Bart answered. Steven continued to probe. At one point, Bart looked at Holly and rolled his eyes. She tried to give him an encouraging smile. Steven looked at her frequently, watching her. She was certain he had been about to ask her out when the ambulance showed up. Would he still do it? She hoped so. But she also felt incredibly confused. With Bart here, she was again aware of her intense attraction to him. She trembled every time her eyes met his. Steven didn't have that effect on her, yet she felt certain she had more in common with him than with Bart.

Steven continued to probe. Holly wished they could hurry up and give Bart something to kill the pain.

"Holly, help superjock here get settled on the table in the X ray room," Steven said at last. "I'll go ahead and get the machine ready." He looked at both of them. "You two know each other well?"

he asked, his voice friendly, though Holly thought she detected a slight note of suspicion in it.

"We have econ class together," she said self-consciously. "That's all." Bart looked at her and smiled slightly, but he didn't say anything.

"The X ray room is right around the corner," she told Bart as Steven left. "Here. Just get off the table slowly and we'll walk over there."

"You look great in a white uniform," Bart said, easing to the floor and beginning to walk beside her.

Holly's blush deepened. She tried not to look at his bare chest. He was muscular, with broad shoulders. She felt light-headed and tingly as she held his good arm and led him down the hall.

Steven came around the corner. "You two need some help? Everything's set up here."

"Sorry," Holly mumbled, sure that Steven could detect her attraction to Bart. "We're hurrying."

Fifteen minutes later, Dr. Ellerbee was examining Bart, the X rays hanging on the lightboard next to him. "You've got what we call a Grade II Acromiclavicular Separation," he said. "That's a fancy term for a shoulder separation. It's a common sports injury, but some special care is needed to heal it or there's a risk of sustaining a really serious injury if it gets hit again."

"How many games will I miss?" Bart asked anxiously.

"I'll get to that. Let me explain this to you first, Bart," Dr. Ellerbee said kindly. "Right now there's a lot of pain and swelling in your left shoulder. You need to keep those ice packs on it the rest of the night, and if the swelling hasn't started going down tomorrow, keep ice on it until it does. It doesn't look to me like there's any real serious damage to the joint," he added, looking closely at the X ray again, "and you're lucky. But — and I know this will be hard for you — you're not going to be playing football for three to five weeks. At least two weeks of that time you're going to have to wear a sling to keep you from moving that shoulder." He peered over his glasses at Bart, who sat quietly on the edge of the examining table, his eyes on the floor. "Any questions?"

"That means I miss the whole middle part of the season. Maybe more." Bart looked at him pleadingly. "You sure I can't speed that up?"

"Three weeks' minimum, with luck," Dr. Ellerbee said. "Sorry, Bart. Other than sports, you're free to do what you want, except you're not going to be able to drive while you have your arm in that sling. We need to monitor the injury closely, so I want you to come back to see me next Thursday after school for another X ray. Right now I'm going to give you some prescription painkillers. They'll make you drowsy, so you need to get home to bed and sleep this off. We got a phone call a few minutes ago from your parents. They're on their way to pick you up."

Dr. Ellerbee chuckled. "That's the first time I've ever spoken to someone calling from one of those car phones. Of course I don't get calls from congressmen every day. It must be pretty exciting having a father who's in the House of Representatives. You're from Montana, right? I was there once. It's a beautiful state."

"Dr. E., sorry to interrupt," Holly said, standing in the doorway of the examining room, "but we just got another call from Bart's father. They've been held up in traffic and it may be another hour before they get here." She glanced at Bart, who was watching her, and smiled sympathetically. Poor Bart! She knew he had received bad news from Dr. Ellerbee and she wished she could do something to help. He had told her that when he left the game things weren't going real well for Kennedy. She still hadn't found out the score.

Dr. Ellerbee frowned. "I think Bart needs to get to bed as soon as he can. There must be a quicker way we can get him home." He looked at her. "Could you drop him off, Holly? It's ten now, your quitting time, and you both live in Rose Hill. Didn't you say the two of you are classmates?"

Holly felt her cheeks grow red and was surprised to see Bart's expression perk up. "Sure. I can give him a ride."

Steven came into the examining room, moving quickly in his usual fashion. "Dr. Ellerbee, another patient just came in. Looks like a minor concussion to me. You'd better take a look. So," he said, turning to Bart, "how's superjock? Think you'll live?" Holly wished Steven would lay off of Bart. He was being awfully obvious about his dislike for him. She could just imagine what he was thinking. Another spoiled rich kid, or part of the privileged elite. She didn't like to think of

68

how she'd have to defend Bart next time she worked with Steven.

Dr. Ellerbee got up and went to the door. "Thanks, Holly. Good luck, Bart. I'll see you Thursday afternoon. Steven," he said, taking his arm, "you come with me. I think Holly can help Bart get dressed and get to her car." He smiled at Holly. "She's going to take our football hero home. Bart, here's your medication. I want you to go ahead and take two of them now."

As Dr. Ellerbee and Steven turned to leave, Holly glanced up and saw Steven looking at her. He had a scowl on his face. For the first time, he didn't seem quite so devastatingly attractive. She was suddenly angry at both guys — at Steven for exposing a side of his personality she didn't find very attractive, and at Bart, whose presence seemed to somehow magnify Steven's flaws.

Chapter 9

Holly turned on the car radio as she and Bart headed home, hoping to catch the final score of the Kennedy-Leesburg game on the local station. She gave Bart a quick sidelong glance. He sat with his hands clenched in tight fists. She knew he was starting to get drowsy from the medication and his shoulder probably still hurt badly. He was wearing his cut-up jersey and had ice packs strapped under it on his shoulder. The sling Dr. Ellerbee had given him was in a small flat box on his lap. Dr. E. had instructed him to wear it during the day.

The traffic was heavy. Holly was driving as carefully as she could, afraid of jarring Bart's shoulder with a quick stop. At the first red light she came to, she leaned down and began fumbling with the knobs of the car's old AM radio. Before the light turned green, she had tuned in the scratchy, faint signal of the local station that featured the high school game of the week.

"The Leesburg-Kennedy game has just ended with Leesburg winning seventeen to fourteen. It was a tough game, hard fought every inch of the way, but it's Leesburg's victory! And that's the report from here at the stadium."

Holly clicked off the radio. They drove in silence for several moments while she searched for something to say. What comfort could she offer? Kennedy had just lost the biggest game of the year, and Bart was going to miss at least the next three games.

"I'm sorry, Bart." Her voice was low and husky, filled with emotion she couldn't control. He glanced at her, his eyelids heavy, then turned his head away and stared out the window.

"You okay?" she asked hesitantly. "Has the medication started to help at all yet?"

He shrugged. "It's not that. I've been injured before. The pain will go away."

Holly waited, while silence filled the car. Finally she spoke. "I guess I'd better get you home. Your parents should be — "

"If I'd been playing, we might have won."

"And we might not have," Holly said quickly. He frowned at her, his eyes full of hurt. "I didn't mean that you wouldn't have made a difference," she said hastily. "I just meant that you can't blame yourself. Football is a team sport. Individuals can make a big difference, but it's not your fault that you got hurt. You can't take responsibility for — "

"Okay, okay, I get the message." Bart chuckled ruefully.

71

It was wonderful to hear him laugh. Holly felt so much better that she laughed a little herself. They both stopped laughing at the same moment, looked at each other in surprise, and then laughed again. Bart started to turn toward her, but twisted his shoulder in the process and gasped in pain. He leaned back in his seat. "Better take it easy. I guess the medication is starting to numb this. I almost forgot about it."

"We'll be home soon," Holly said.

"It's just a football game. I know that," Bart said, sounding as if he was trying to convince himself of what he was saying. "Leesburg is tough. They played a good game. We'll rebound."

"Right," Holly said encouragingly. "Besides, if you don't take that attitude, you're dead in the water. You're out for a few weeks and that's that, so you're going to have to be philosophical about this."

He had given her his home address and she had no trouble finding the house. She had a clear picture of it in her mind before she ever saw it, a picture that had formed that morning when she was talking to Diana on the phone. It was in one of the nicest sections of Rose Hill, on a beautiful winding street. The house itself was a two-story colonial of white brick with tall columns in the front and a sweeping lawn shaded by graceful old willow trees. As she turned into the circular drive she saw a pale yellow Lincoln Continental pull up behind them.

As Holly stopped her car, a woman wearing a formal gown got out of the other car and ran over to them. A handsome, distinguished-looking man in a tuxedo followed behind her. Holly was struck by Bart's resemblance to his father: They were both tall and dark, with the same square jaw and rugged good looks.

"Oh, Bart, are you okay?" the woman asked as they got out of the car. She gazed anxiously at her son. His father hovered in front of them with his hands in his pockets, apparently unsure of what he should do. "Sorry we couldn't get to the clinic to pick you up, Bart. The traffic was terrible."

"It's okay, Dad," Bart said. "Holly didn't mind bringing me home. Holly?" He turned and signaled to her to come over.

Embarrassed, she moved around the car and stood next to them. "Hi, I'm Holly Daniels," she said nervously, extending a hand. "I know Diana and Bart from school."

Mrs. Einerson smiled at her. "Thank you for bringing Bart home, dear. I can't tell you how upset I was that we couldn't get over to pick him up. At least we had the phone in the car so we could call." She turned to Bart. "You look so pale, darling. Let's go into the house."

With his parents on either side of him, Bart moved slowly toward the front door. Holly didn't know what to do and stood awkwardly in the driveway. As Mrs. Einerson opened the door, they could hear the sound of the phone ringing. She moved ahead to answer it, and Holly quickly stepped next to Bart to offer support if necessary. She could tell that he needed to lie down — the medication had made him so groggy he was having trouble walking.

"I'll take him on up to his room," Mr. Einerson said to Holly. "Thank you again for your help. Here we go, Bart," he said tenderly.

"Wait a minute, Dad." Bart turned to Holly. His eyes looked glazed. She knew he would be asleep as soon as his head hit the pillow. "Thanks a lot, Holly." He smiled slightly. "I wanted to see where you work, but I can guarantee you I didn't get hurt in the game for that reason."

Holly smiled and gave a little wave and watched Mr. Einerson put his arm around Bart's waist and carefully walk him up the elegant staircase. As she moved toward the front door, she could hear Mrs. Einerson on the kitchen phone. "I'm sorry, dear, say your name again, would you? Heather? Your father is who? Oh yes, of course we know who he is. Yes, I'll tell Bart you called. Oh that's nice of you, dear, but he really can't come to the phone. Not tonight. Yes, I'll tell him to call you tomorrow."

Holly slipped outside. Heather. Was something going on between the two of them? If Mrs. Einerson didn't know who she was, then it didn't seem likely that Bart went out with Heather. But he sure acted like he liked her, and it was obvious to everyone how she felt about him.

Not that it was really important to Holly what girl Bart Einerson was dating.

As Holly climbed into her car, she noticed the stars above her twinkling in a deep blue-black sky, and she smiled to herself, remembering the ride with Bart and the way he had laughed in the car. She had to admit it: For all his shortcomings, there was something about him that was irresistible to her. She certainly could say she didn't know anyone else like him. But she had to keep reminding herself he wasn't for her. He was a flirt, not the kind of boy she could take seriously.

She started the engine and drove away, a wave of confusion sweeping over her. Forget Bart and think about Steven. He had been so funny tonight, teasing her and joking with her.

And if it hadn't been for the arrival of the ambulance with Bart, he might have asked her out. Steven shared her values and her ambitions. Whatever she felt for Bart, she needed to get over it. He wasn't for her. But somehow, thoughts of him kept lingering in the back of her mind.

Chapter
10

John Marquette turned off the lights of the old pickup he was driving and looked cautiously around the commons of the Leesburg campus. He turned to Ed Owens and Bernie Hays, who sat stone-faced in the front seat with him. "Think everybody's asleep?" he asked in a husky whisper.

Ed and Bernie peered through the windshield. "Guess so," Ed shrugged. "I don't see anybody." He looked at his watch. "It's almost three A.M., so they should be."

They sat in silence for several moments, looking out the windows. In front of them, the statue of Robert E. Lee loomed majestically toward the sky. It had been fully restored since the pink paint incident a year ago.

This year Ted Mason had turned chicken. John couldn't believe it when Ted refused to come along tonight. All of a sudden he'd become a wimp who wouldn't even get involved in a little harmless fun. And what really made John mad was that Ted had convinced most of the other players not to come along to get revenge on Leesburg for Kennedy's humiliating 17-14 defeat that night. At least Ed and Bernie were real men. *Someone* had to get revenge on Leesburg for what had happened on the football field.

Of course, John would have come tonight even if Kennedy had won. In that case, they would have just been adding delicious insult to humiliating injury. But since Kennedy lost, it was more important than ever that somebody from Kennedy do something to the Leesburg campus, and it looked like he — with Ed and Bernie's help, of course — was the only one brave enough to make sure it got done.

His revenge was perfect. The Leesburg campus was always so pristine, with its award-winning landscaping that the cadets all helped to take care of and took such pride in. What greater insult to the eye than to come out of their dorms in the morning to find the whole central campus strewn with garbage. The day before the game, John and his two friends had each collected several bags of trash and loaded them in the back of John's sister's pickup truck.

The crowning touch was the sign he had made to hang on the statue of General Lee. He could just see the cadets stumbling through the garbage to read it. And what message would their infamous general be proclaiming to them? TAKE IT FROM ME, LEESBURG STINKS! John chuckled just thinking of the looks on their faces. It would be the best prank he ever pulled off. And boy, would it be a *mess* trying to clean up all that stuff! Just to make it extra difficult, he had watered down everything so none of the trash would blow away. It would take them hours to clean up and would be one of the most unpleasant jobs imaginable. He'd give anything to be able to be there to watch.

"I wonder how Bart is doing," murmered Ed. "You shouldn't have jumped on him like that, Marquette."

John whipped around angrily. "Hey! I didn't start that pile-up. You can't blame that on me."

"Yeah, but you didn't have to add to it. It was all over by then, and you could tell that Bart was wide open when you jumped," Ed shot back.

"Shhh," Bernie cautioned them. "Let's not argue about it. Bart's gonna be okay."

"Well, it's going to be rough next week without him. He's the best end we've got. We sure needed him tonight."

"He's a wimp!" John growled. "He thinks he's Mr. Hot-Shot because his dad's a congressman. I can't stand those sissy boots he wears and that phony smile he's always using on everybody."

"C'mon, Marquette, we all know you're still mad because his sister turned you down. It wasn't Bart's fault that Diana flipped for that British guy."

"Yeah!" huffed John. "He's another one! A wimp with a camera. Always snapping pictures."

"Come on, guys, if we're going to get this done, let's get started before somebody sees us," Bernie pleaded. "The sooner we're out of here, the better. So let's go, okay?"

John and Ed nodded and the three boys quietly got out of the pickup. For the next half hour they worked swiftly, strewing the reeking bags of garbage around the lawn surrounding the statue. While Ed and Bernie finished the last two bags, John climbed up the statue and hung his sign, laughing to himself as he slipped it over General Lee's head. This was just too good for words! Too bad he hadn't thought to bring a camera along. He could have submitted the picture to Sasha Jenkins with a note suggesting she run it on the front page of *The Red and the Gold*.

She was another person who always had her nose in the air, thinking she was so special. John had been trying for two years to get her to go out with him. But now she went with some college student and wouldn't even give him the time of day.

"C'mon, Marquette. We gotta get out of here!" Ed hissed from the base of the statue. "Bernie thinks he saw someone near one of those buildings over there. Hurry up!"

John adjusted the sign and climbed down the statue. He looked around at the littered lawn and almost laughed out loud. The garbage was everywhere! They'd even made sure to get it tangled into the shrubbery and flowers.

The three boys hopped into the pickup truck and John started the motor. Then he couldn't hold it in any longer and began to laugh. Ed and Bernie joined him, and the three of them roared out loud, oblivious to everything else.

Suddenly Ed stopped and hushed the other

two. "Did you hear something?" he asked, his voice scared.

"Naw, you just got the creeps," Bernie assured him. "But come on, Marquette, let's get out of here."

John swung the pickup around, and as he did so, the boys saw two dark, silent cars blocking their way. Suddenly the cars' headlights glared on, and sirens began to screech, and lights to flash. Before John, Ed, or Bernie could think of anything else, four police officers were approaching the pickup.

Chapter
11

A car honking behind her startled Holly, bringing her back to reality. Driving in busy Saturday afternoon traffic was no time to be daydreaming about her date that night with Steven.

He had called her at ten that morning to ask her to a movie, and she had immediately accepted. When the phone rang, she and her mother were just starting breakfast and she was telling her mom about Bart's injury. Ever since Steven's call, she had been walking on a cloud.

Signaling left, she turned onto Federal Boulevard, carefully pacing herself with the other cars on the crowded roadway. Her mother had asked her to pick up some groceries and run a few errands, and she had finally finished. It was a warm fall day and she was thirsty. Up ahead she saw the sub shop and decided to stop. A soft drink would taste good on the drive home.

As she ordered a 7-Up at the counter, she

heard a familiar voice behind her. "Hey, Holly, what are you up to?" She waved at Phoebe, who was sitting at a table with Sasha Jenkins and Chris Austin.

"Come join us!" Phoebe called to her. "Do you have time?"

Holly hesitated. She still didn't feel like these were her friends, but the three girls looked so friendly, and she did want to get to know them better. Sasha and Phoebe smiled at her, and Chris moved her purse off the empty seat so Holly could sit down.

She took a deep breath and walked over to their table. "Thanks," she said, smiling at them as she slipped in next to Chris. "I still have a few minutes before I have to be home."

"We were talking about what happened last night. Have you heard?" Phoebe asked.

"Heard what?"

"John Marquette, Bernie Hays, and Ed Owens were caught by the police on the Leesburg campus. They were taken to the police station and their parents had to come get them. Boy, are they in trouble!"

"What did they do?" Holly asked.

"They trashed the Leesburg campus," Sasha announced. "And I mean *trashed*. They dumped bagloads of garbage all over the beautiful lawns out there. Can you believe how immature they are?"

"How'd they get caught?"

"We're not sure," Phoebe said. "Somebody must have seen them and called the police."

"Wow," Holly whistled. "Three first-string

football players. We heard John say yesterday that he planned to do something, remember, Phoebe? Leesburg was probably ready and waiting. What happens now?"

"We don't know," Phoebe said nonchalantly. "They were allowed to go home with their parents last night — or I should say this morning. I guess it happened about three A.M."

"I hope something *severe* happens to them," Chris said angrily. "This really makes Kennedy High look bad. Especially after that dumb stunt last year. Our school is going to get a bad reputation."

"I agree," Sasha said seriously. "I'm going to write an editorial about it for next Friday's edition of *The Red and the Gold*. Leesburg didn't do anything to us after last year's incident, and a lot of people think that they have better sportsmanship than we do. Like Chris said, it makes Kennedy look bad."

"At least Ted wasn't involved this year," Chris said. "Maybe he's finally growing up, but I guess Marquette never will. If those three guys get suspended from the team for this, we'll be in big trouble, but I think they deserve it. Too bad Bart will be out, too."

Holly looked up at the mention of Bart's name. As hard as she had tried not to think about him, she had found him in her thoughts throughout the day. He had some kind of hold on her that was totally unfamiliar to her and that she didn't understand. "How is Bart today? Does anybody know?" she asked, trying to sound casual.

"I heard he had a pretty rough night," Chris

said. "My sister talked to Diana this morning."

"The first twenty-four hours are always hard when you have a Grade II separation," Holly said quickly. "After that, the swelling goes down pretty fast and the tenderness gradually goes away. Bart didn't have any complications with his injury, so he should heal without problems."

The three girls stared at her. "How do you know all that?" Phoebe asked. "You sound like you've seen Bart's shoulder."

"I have," Holly murmured, embarrassed. "I was working at the clinic last night when he was brought in. I gave him a ride home."

"So the injury isn't too serious?"

"He has to wear a sling for a couple of weeks and he was told he would miss at least three games — but he shouldn't have any long-term problems."

"You sound like a doctor," Chris said admiringly.

"I want to be a nurse someday. I've always loved medicine."

"Oh boy, do I remember!" Phoebe laughed. "You and I used to play hospital by the hour when we were kids and you always made me be the patient. Remember the time we wrapped the cat's leg with surgical tape? The poor thing — we almost killed him getting it off!"

"And the 'medicine' we made that we bribed your little brother to drink. We're lucky we *didn't* kill him," Holly said, making everyone laugh.

As the girls continued to chat, Holly began to relax. She felt like she could be good friends with all of them, but she felt especially drawn to Phoebe, with her vibrant red hair and sparkling green eyes, because of the connection in their past.

"I can't wait to meet Jeremy's sister, Fiona," Sasha said suddenly, sipping her club soda. "I'll bet she's tall and thin and wears leotards all the time since she's a ballerina. If she starts school at Kennedy I can interview her for the paper."

"Maybe we can fix her up with Ted for the costume party," Phoebe suggested.

"I don't think he's too interested in going out with anyone right now," Sasha said. "At least, that's what he told me."

"Maybe she'll hit it off with Bart," Chris said. "Since his sister goes out with Jeremy, it would be a natural."

Holly felt a stab of jealousy, just as she did whenever she pictured Heather and Bart together. She couldn't understand her reaction. How could she be so excited about her date with Steven, and yet be unable to stop thinking about Bart? She kept reminding herself he was nothing more than a flirt, but somehow she couldn't get him out of her mind.

"If you fix Fiona up with Bart, you'll have to ask Heather Richardson for permission," Phoebe said sarcastically. "Can you believe the way she acts around him? Kim told me that when Bart got hurt last night, Heather was hanging around the locker room trying to find out how he was."

"It is incredible the way she throws herself at him," Sasha added. "So what's up for tonight, Pheeb?"

"I'm going to the movies with Chris and Greg and Michael. You want to come?"

Sasha sighed. "No, I think I'll just stay home. That's the problem with a boyfriend who goes to college in another town — you spend a lot of nights at home. How about you, Holly? Do you have any plans?"

Holly smiled. "I'm going out with a guy named Steven who works at the clinic. Our first date."

"You look pleased," Chris teased.

"I've been hoping he would ask."

"I thought maybe you were interested in Bart after I saw you with him at lunch yesterday," Phoebe said, confused.

"We're just friends," Holly said quickly. "Remember, I told you we're in the same econ small group."

"Oh, that's right." Phoebe sounded disappointed.

"The worst date I ever had was last year when I got conned into going out with John Marquette," Sasha said, shuddering. "I was supposed to conduct an interview with him over dinner, but he wouldn't say a word until he got me into his cousin's apartment. What a night!"

"We all had our ups and downs with romance last year," Chris laughed, looking at Phoebe and Sasha. "Notice how we've all settled down as seniors? I wonder what will happen in college next year."

Phoebe frowned. "Michael and I will probably go to different colleges. It's really going to be hard, but we each have to go to the school that's right for us."

"Being apart is hard," Sasha agreed, "but what's nice about it is that when you get together, you're so happy to see each other. I can't wait until Rob gets here for the party next Saturday night. I haven't seen him for three whole weeks!"

"Since Greg is two grades behind me, we'll be separated, too," Chris said, her blue eyes sad. "I guess it'll be a good test for us, but it'll be so hard to leave him behind. I just feel lucky I met him when I did. At least we'll have this year together."

"That's the way I feel, too," Phoebe said. "I never would have thought when I first met Michael that we would be right for each other, but the more I got to know him, the more I knew that I loved him. You're the one who told me to listen to my heart instead of my head, Sasha. Just like you've done with Rob."

Holly looked at the three girls and smiled. "I wish I could participate in this discussion. Maybe you have to be a senior to be in love."

"No way! We were *all* in love last year," Phoebe said. "We just weren't in love with the right guys. *That* doesn't happen until you're a senior," she teased.

Chris went up to the counter and returned a minute later with a bag of cheese curls, which she set in the middle of the table. "Monica told me she and Peter were going to come to the costume party as Tarzan and Jane. She said Peter has read every one of the Tarzan books."

"I'm surprised he didn't pick a more literary character. He's always reading," Sasha commented.

"How many people do you expect?" Holly asked.

"Fifty at last count. I'm afraid it's going to be too crowded," Sasha said worriedly. "Mom and Dad don't mind, but we don't want to be packed in there like sardines. It'll get hot with costumes on!"

"Peter and Monica won't be hot in their loin-cloths," joked Chris.

The other girls laughed. "You're coming, aren't you, Holly?" Sasha asked.

"Well — "

"Oh, come," Phoebe said. "Everyone will be there."

"If I can get off work, I'll definitely come. It really sounds like fun."

"Bring Steven if you want to."

Holly considered for a moment. "I don't think he would come," she frowned.

"Why not?" Phoebe asked.

"He's — not the type." She looked at Phoebe pleadingly. "You know what I mean."

Phoebe shrugged. "I guess so. Well, just so long as you come."

"I wouldn't miss it," she said warmly, looking around at these three girls who were now her friends.

At home, Holly found a note from her mother saying she had gone to visit a friend and would be back at six. She put the groceries away, then paced restlessly through the quiet house, her mind racing. She felt surprisingly unsettled, in spite of the way things were going. She was making friends, and Steven had asked her out. But something just didn't feel right. Only a few days earlier, the knowledge that Steven wouldn't be caught at something like a high school costume party had been part of his attraction. Now she was disappointed that he wasn't the kind of guy who would share things like that with her.

She pictured Steven at Sasha's party. He would analyze each of her friends, telling her what was wrong with them and stereotyping them as rich and spoiled. She would spend the whole evening defending them. She didn't know Steven that well, but she knew that's what would happen. She frowned. If only Steven would give people a chance! He was so quick to jump to conclusions. She knew her friends would give him a chance. They were open and friendly and went out of their way to make others feel comfortable. They had proven that yesterday on the quad with her and in their discussion about helping Jeremy's sister Fiona. But Steven wouldn't extend the same courtesy to them.

The way he had treated Bart last night at the clinic was typical of the way he often reacted to people. He no sooner met them than he made a judgment, and what he decided determined how he treated them. But there were a lot of things she liked about him, too, she reminded herself.

But as she tried to recall them, her thoughts drifted to Bart. Chris had said he had had a bad night. How much was the shoulder bothering him? And how was he feeling now about Kennedy High losing the game last night? He had been so hard on himself and he was in such pain that she had badly wanted to comfort him.

She could call him. It seemed like a reasonable thing to do, to simply inquire about how he was getting along. She paced around her bedroom, then finally looked up the number. Her hands shook. Why was this so hard?

"Hello." Holly was relieved to hear Diana's voice.

She sucked in her breath. "Hi, Diana. It's Holly. I just called — well, actually, to see how Bart is doing."

"Lots better! Thanks for bringing him home last night. We all really appreciate that. I was stuck at the stadium. You should have seen me frantically trying to find my parents. They were at some reception and were pretty hard to get ahold of. Guess what happened a few minutes ago?"

"I wouldn't know where to start," Holly said.

"Do you know who Heather Richardson is?"

Holly's hands suddenly felt clammy. "Yeah, I have a class with her."

"She came over here. Can you believe that? She brought Bart *flowers*. My mother was pretty impressed."

"Was Bart — impressed?" Holly asked, her throat dry. She swallowed hard.

"He's not here. He and Ted and some of the other guys went to the Georgetown football game. They left an hour ago. We didn't know if Bart should go, but he said he felt pretty good, and Ted promised to watch out for him. Heather was *real* disappointed that he wasn't home. I can't believe how she's chasing him. When she found out where he went, she said her dad had box seats and she was going to get him to take her to the game. She left right away. You should have seen her sweet-talking my mom. Too bad Bart missed it."

"Yeah. He would have enjoyed it," Holly said sarcastically.

"Did you hear about what happened at Leesburg last night?"

"I think it's terrible."

"Me, too. Bart said he wasn't surprised. What a stupid thing to do. Bart's worried that all three of them might get kicked off the team, which is what they deserve, but we'd be in pretty bad shape if that happened."

"But Bart's better today?"

"He says he is. He's never one to tell you when he isn't okay. I've had the feeling some things have been bothering him lately, but I can't get him to talk. If I ever say anything, he always says everything's great. He insisted he was well enough to go to the Georgetown game. Ted drove and he promised to bring Bart home if his shoulder started hurting too much."

After she hung up, Holly tried to sort out her thoughts. She found out what she wanted to know — that Bart was doing okay. She also found out that Heather brought him flowers.

Oh, well. None of it mattered to Holly anyway. In a few hours she would be on her first date with Steven. Dreamy, tall, handsome Steven. She couldn't think any more about Bart. Tonight just might be the best night of her life!

Chapter 12

When the waitress left after taking their order, Steven smiled across the table at Holly. "So you weren't crazy about the movie, huh?"

"It seemed so violent," Holly said hesitantly. She wished she could think of something more sophisticated to say. The truth was that she hated the film, but she knew he had liked it. She didn't want him to think she couldn't take the violence, although the movie had been so repulsive she wasn't sure she really cared what he thought. If she hadn't been with him, she would have walked out shortly after it began.

"You've got to have some escapism from time to time," Steven laughed. "That's why people go to that kind of movie."

"But it was so pointless. Why let us get all involved in the characters and then see them torn apart or crushed to death or something?" Holly shook her head. "I just don't get it."

"I guess you have to be older," Steven teased.

But Holly didn't feel like joking. "I hope I never like films like that," she shuddered. "If you have to be older, then I guess I'll stay young."

"Hey, I was just kidding," Steven said defensively. "Maybe it's my upbringing. When you come from Brooklyn, it takes a lot to get you good and repulsed."

Holly didn't know whether to take him seriously or not, but figured he must think this was funny, so she laughed. She wanted to drop the subject of the movie. It had made her uncomfortable. She couldn't understand how someone like Steven, who planned to be a doctor and devote his career to healing the sick and caring for the injured, could get such a kick out of all that blood and gore.

He was still watching her with a scrutinizing expression on his face and she looked away. She should probably laugh it off, make jokes about the movie and just enjoy being with Steven, but she was finding it difficult to talk to him and she wasn't enjoying herself. Kidding around at the clinic was one thing — spending an evening together was turning out to be something else. At the clinic he seemed older, responsible, and more desirable than he did now. Out of the white doctor's jacket, wearing a knit shirt and slacks, he seemed, well, ordinary.

She wanted the evening to be over — which surprised her since she had wanted to go out with Steven ever since she had met him. But now she just wanted to be back in her own bedroom. She needed time to think through what had happened because her reaction to him confused her.

She was afraid he knew how she felt and she thought she knew how he felt. He probably wanted the evening over, too. He probably was wondering why he ever asked her out. He probably thought she was naive and boring.

The waitress brought their hamburgers and French fries and for a few minutes they ate in silence.

"Maybe we should have found an old Charlie Chaplin flick to go to," Steven said between mouthfuls.

She glanced at him, her cheeks turning red. "I've seen them all," she said, "but I always love seeing one again."

"Next time we go out," Steven smiled, "let me know where there's one playing."

Holly didn't respond. She wasn't sure she wanted a next time. The things that had first attracted her to Steven — his good looks, his interest in medicine, his easygoing nature — hadn't changed. The evening just wasn't turning out the way she had expected, and his narrow-mindedness was really getting to her. A group of Kennedy High students were at the movie and had acted crazy while they watched it. Steven made several cutting remarks about them, calling them spoiled and rich and immature high school kids. Holly wanted to point out that any normal person would react to the movie the way they had. They weren't the ones who were out of line — the *movie* was.

She felt all evening like she had to act sophisticated. She couldn't let herself act silly and just have a good time or he would say something sarcastic to her. Sasha seemed to do fine dating a college student, but it wasn't working out for her.

But Holly knew the problem wasn't that Steven was a college student. The problem was Steven. They weren't enough alike. Whatever physical attraction she had felt for him was gone. Phoebe had said that afternoon that you have to follow your heart. Choosing Steven had been an intellectual decision. Holly had thought that they were well suited to each other. Her heart had its own ideas. There was another boy her heart yearned for, and she knew it — a boy her intellect rejected. A boy named Bart.

At the door an hour later, Holly knew Steven was going to kiss her good-night. When he did so, she stood there passively, not responding to his embrace. "Hey, relax, Holly," Steven said half-jokingly. "I'm not going to bite you."

"Sorry," she mumbled.

"Let's do something next Saturday night," he suggested.

"I can't. I have plans."

"Oh? Doing what?"

"I've been invited to a Halloween party. With my high school friends." She held her breath, waiting to see how he would respond to that. Phoebe had urged her to invite him.

Steven made a face. "Wouldn't you rather go to a movie?"

"No. I'm really looking forward to this party."

"I suppose you'll bob for apples and feel peeled

grapes and think they're eyeballs and things like that, right?"

She laughed. "I hope so. That sounds like fun."

"You're putting me on," he said incredulously. "You don't really want to do that kind of stuff, do you?"

"Don't forget that I'm still in high school," Holly said, her eyes twinkling mischievously. "Thanks for a nice evening, Steven."

He shrugged. "Okay, good-night, Holly. See you at work this week."

When he turned and left, Holly breathed a sigh of relief and hurried inside, reveling in the feeling of freedom that washed over her. She was glad he was gone. What had she ever seen in him in the first place? How come she hadn't realized that he was so opinionated? And that movie! Why would he have taken her to see something like that! Never again. From now on, she'd let it be known up front that she wouldn't go to a movie like that, and he could think anything he wanted to about her.

She pulled off her clothes and put on her nightshirt and found her thoughts drifting to Bart. Somehow she knew he wouldn't have taken her to such a film.

"But he probably would have flirted with every girl in the restaurant," she mumbled to herself. "Once a flirt, always a flirt." No guy who would encourage a girl like Heather Richardson to keep coming on to him was the kind of guy who would change his ways for someone like Holly.

She willed herself not to think about Bart, but she couldn't get him out of her thoughts. Her mind went over and over the way he had smiled at her in class, the way she felt when she was next to him.

She sighed. Why weren't there any easy answers? Why did her heart and mind have to fight each other like this? Why couldn't she forget about both Steven *and* Bart?

As she lay in bed trying to get to sleep, there was only one thing she knew for sure: It was easy to forget about Steven, but she couldn't wait to see Bart again at school on Monday.

Chapter
13

When Holly walked into Ms. Tyler's classroom late Monday morning, she took a seat by herself and got out her notebook, her hands shaking in anticipation as she waited for Bart to appear.

When he did a moment later, she pretended to be busy getting her notes organized. He stopped at the doorway to talk to Gene Watkins. Holly held her breath.

And then, what she was wishing for happened. He sat down next to her. Her heart was beating so loudly she was sure he must be able to hear it. His left arm was in the sling Dr. Ellerbee had given him. He didn't act like his shoulder was bothering him, but she knew it must have been sore.

"Hope you don't mind if I sit here," Bart said, his voice friendly.

She gave him a quick smile. "Of course not.

How are you feeling?" She still wasn't breathing naturally.

"A lot better, thanks."

"Did you get along okay yesterday?"

"Yeah, I was careful. The medication helps a lot. It's a drag not being able to drive, but worse not being able to play football. You probably heard about Marquette. The team might be in big trouble."

"You mean if he's suspended?"

Bart let out a loud sigh. "Yeah. Rumors are flying. Four of us off the team would be tough."

She wanted to ask about the Georgetown football game and whether Heather had shown up. But if she asked what he did Saturday night, he might ask her the same thing.

"What did you do Saturday night?"

Startled, Holly looked at him. "Saturday night? I — I had a date."

"Oh." Bart started to open his economics book, then grinned at her. "I didn't mean to be snoopy. It's none of my business. I just wondered. So — who was your date with?"

She laughed nervously. "Why do you want to know?"

"Just curious," he said innocently, his eyes twinkling.

"His name is Steven. He's the one who first examined your shoulder at the clinic."

"I could tell he liked you," Bart said casually. "All I did this weekend was go to a lousy football game. Georgetown got creamed."

Holly tried to think of a way to ask about Heather but she didn't have the nerve.

Ms. Tyler started class by taking roll. When she came to Bart, she smiled and asked how he was. It was clear that she thought a lot of him. In fact, all of the students in the class seemed to respect Bart. As always he was prepared for class discussion. Listening to him express an opinion on the Federal Reserve System, Holly resolved to start studying her economics harder. She needed to if she was ever going to keep up with him.

She wondered if he was going to the costume party Saturday night. Dr. Ellerbee had already agreed that if she worked Friday night — which meant missing another football game — she could count on Saturday night off for the party.

What to wear was the next problem. She wanted to go as a nurse, but she couldn't come up with many interesting nurses in literature — with one exception: Catherine Barkley in Ernest Hemingway's novel *A Farewell to Arms*. She had found an old-fashioned nurse's uniform, but she was having trouble finding a blue cape and nurse's cap. She already had white tights and shoes.

"I've been able to complete the arrangements for your interviews with government economists," Ms. Tyler was saying. "As I told you before, these have been set up for next Wednesday and Thursday. You all have permission from the office to be away from school one of those afternoons. Here's the list."

Holly quickly scanned the sheet she was handed. For a moment she couldn't believe her eyes. She and Bart were assigned to the same team! They were to meet with Mr. Barston

Everett on Thursday afternoon at three P.M. at his office at the Department of Energy on the Washington Mall. Then she realized she couldn't go on Thursday. She had to work at the clinic. With a sinking feeling she raised her hand.

"I have work release on Thursdays, Ms. Tyler," she said. "I start at noon that day and don't finish until three, so I would be late. I'd better switch to a Wednesday interview."

Ms. Tyler looked thoughtful. "I don't think the drive to Mr. Everett's office would take more than twenty minutes from the clinic," she said. "If you have your own car, why don't you just join us a little late? That way we can keep the schedule like it is."

Holly smiled. "That would be fine. Thanks!"

"Bart, you have a question?" Ms. Tyler asked, nodding to him.

"I have a scheduling problem, too. I'm supposed to get my shoulder x-rayed at the same clinic at two o'clock. I was treated by a doctor there after Friday night's game and the appointment was all set up."

"I see no reason to change it," Ms. Tyler said. "If you can catch a ride over to the clinic for your appointment, why don't you just come with Holly to the interview? Would that be okay, Holly?"

She nodded, her heart pounding.

This time she waited for Bart at the end of class. "I thought your appointment with Dr. E. was later in the afternoon," she teased as they walked down the hall.

"Yeah, but I don't want to miss the interview," he smiled. "Don't you think he'd be willing to see me a little early?"

Holly laughed. "I'm sure there will be no problem."

"You don't mind being my chauffeur again?"

"Nope. But you *will* owe me return services once your arm heals, you know."

"It will be my pleasure, madame," Bart said, giving her a grand bow.

"Hey! An impressive gesture!" yelled Woody as he passed them in the hallway. "We could use you in our next drama production, Einerson."

"Just let me know when tryouts are," laughed Bart. "I'll be there." He turned to Holly. "Come have lunch with me."

"Outside? Okay. I have a short lunch period today, so we'd better hurry." Holly was exhilarated. She had been hoping Bart would suggest they go to the quad together.

"Hi, Bart," said a sultry voice.

Holly's heart sank. Heather was standing by the doors to the quad, a girl friend on each side of her. She was wearing bright red stretch pants and a form-fitting gray patterned turtleneck sweater.

"How's your arm?" she asked sweetly, moving up to him. Before he could answer, she turned to Holly, greeting her as though they were best friends. When she was done she turned back to Bart and fingered his sling. "Did you get my flowers? You didn't call and tell me. Your mother said you would," she pouted.

Bart flashed his irresistible grin at her. "Sorry.

The flowers were great. That's the first time I ever got flowers from a girl."

As Holly watched them, she realized that Heather couldn't be blamed for continuing to throw herself at Bart. He wasn't doing anything to discourage it. He smiled at her and was receptive to all her comments and body language. Holly felt invisible and hurt. She knew in a moment Heather would leave and Bart would focus his attention on her again, but that didn't make her feel any better.

Her common sense told her not to be taken in by Bart's charm and good looks. Her heart and mind were in conflict again, but she would resist. How could he be so thoughtful and friendly, and then turn around and ignore her? Any boy who could be so inconsiderate of the girl he was with was bad news. Holly knew the smartest thing she could do was to run in the opposite direction before she ended up with a broken heart.

Chapter
14

Holly was so mixed-up about Bart that for a minute she thought about trying to leave. But they were already walking onto the quad into the warm sunshine, and she didn't want to cause a scene.

His behavior didn't make sense. He had invited her to have lunch with him and then he went ahead and flirted with every girl in sight. Holly couldn't deny that she was more strongly attracted to him than any boy she had ever known — but this one thing drove a terrible wedge between them. Was he interested in Heather or not? If he wasn't, then why did he lead her on? If he was, then why was he leading *Holly* on?

"A penny for your thoughts," Bart said softly, looking into her eyes. "Something the matter?"

"No, it's just that — " But how could she say "It's just that you flirt with Heather"? After all, they were just friends. Holly had to be careful not to interpret their relationship in any other way. They had never gone out together, never exchanged a kiss or any words of affection. She had no right to be jealous. But she was.

"It's just what?" he asked, sounding concerned.

"Nothing." She smiled at him and shrugged her shoulders. "Just a little problem I'm trying to get worked out."

As they joined the crowd, everyone was talking about John Marquette and the incident at Leesburg. Bart and Holly sat down next to Janie. She was wearing a silver-blue dress that Henry had designed and everyone was admiring it. "So when will the three of them be back in school?" Janie asked Michael.

"Maybe Ted knows. I haven't heard a thing." Michael shrugged. He and Phoebe were sharing a lunch of sandwiches and fruit she had prepared and had set up on the grass, complete with red checkered napkins. Phoebe had her back propped against Woody, who was sitting on the grass with Kim. She waved at Holly.

"I don't know, either," Ted said. He was sitting next to Sasha, who was busy writing a letter to Rob and not paying any attention to anything else. They had already finished their lunches. "None of them are here today," Ted added. "I heard Coach Briggs went to talk to their parents. We'll probably hear something by the end of the day."

Holly sat down on a bench next to Bart. She pulled her lunch from her backpack and began to eat. As Bart started eating his sandwich, he nudged her. "Here comes my sister." Holly looked up to see Diana, Jeremy, and a thin, graceful girl walking across the quad.

"That must be Fiona," Phoebe commented.

"You can tell she's a dancer by the way she moves," Kim said.

Fiona Stone was wearing a clingy, rose-colored knit dress that showed off her slender figure. Her short dark blonde hair was swept gracefully off her face. She had big expressive eyes and long lashes. She looked delicate, very feminine, and shy. She smiled sweetly to everyone she was introduced to, but didn't say much.

Diana came over and sat down next to Holly. "Hi! Math class was unreal today. I can't believe that assignment he gave us. Is that my bozo brother with you?" she asked with mock surprise.

Bart laughed. "Thanks for the friendly greeting, Di. So that's Fiona, huh?"

"Yes. She just arrived yesterday. I think she's pretty nervous about being here."

"It is kind of overwhelming," Holly said. "You and I know what it's like to be new, and it's just something you have to work through."

"I think she's a little more comfortable with boys," Diana said hesitantly. "I mean, she's nice to everybody, but she seems to talk more easily with boys. I think she's sort of intimidated by American girls. I hope nobody gets the wrong idea and thinks she's flirting. That could cause problems for her."

"I know what you mean," Holly said thoughtfully. What a perfect opportunity to drop a hint to Bart. She glanced over at him. "What can really cause problems is if you're with someone and someone else comes along and you flirt with them. The person you're with can get pretty upset, even if you don't mean anything by the flirting."

"I see a lot of guys do that sort of thing," Diana agreed.

"I've never noticed it," Bart said.

Diana rolled her eyes. "That's because you're blind."

"You do it, Bart," Holly said softly.

Bart stared at her. "I do?"

Holly's cheeks burned. "Well, you — "

"You flirt with every girl in school," Diana interrupted. "It's true, Bart."

"Oh, come on, I do not!" Bart said angrily.

Holly was shocked. Could Bart really be so unaware of his own habits?

Jeremy and Fiona came over to them. As Jeremy introduced Fiona to Bart, she shyly touched his sling. "What happened to you? Were you in an accident?" she asked politely.

Bart glanced self-consciously at Holly and Diana. "I injured my shoulder in Friday night's football game," he said, acting more flustered than Holly had ever seen him. Poor Bart. Anything he said now would be interpreted as flirting.

"It must hurt terribly. How awful for you," Fiona said.

Diana came to Bart's rescue. "Holly's new at school this year, too. We're in the same math class. Hey, you'll be able to come to your first Kennedy High football game this Friday night, only you won't get to see Bart play."

The loudspeakers on the mall suddenly came

to life, blaring forth the music that introduced Peter Lacey's noontime show. His familiar melodious voice came over the speaker, causing everyone to either talk louder in order to be heard over him, or to stop talking in order to hear him. Bart looked gratefully at the speaker near them and pretended to listen intently. Holly and Diana exchanged knowing looks and Holly smiled to herself. Maybe between the two of them they could point out to Bart what a flirt he was. He probably had always been totally unaware of it. It was just his nature. But she hoped that he could change.

Holly watched Fiona for a moment. She could tell that Jeremy's sister was very sweet, just as Diana had said. Coming into a new school was always hard, as she knew only too well, but Fiona would quickly learn to be comfortable with American girls as well as with the boys. Holly resolved to do whatever she could to help her.

As Peter's first song ended, he came back on the air. "Okay, Cardinals, listen up, because we've got some important news today. Coach Briggs has asked for several minutes of air time. Please give him your attention."

The mall became so quiet that the only sound to be heard was the flag rippling in the gentle breeze. Coach Briggs, who had a raspy voice, cleared his throat as he took the microphone.

"Good afternoon to all of you," he began. "Everyone is sorry we lost our game to Leesburg last Friday. Losing Bart Einerson in the first quarter was a real blow, and we ran into more bad luck late in the game."

Holly looked around, almost expecting Heather to materialize at the mention of Bart's name. Diana reached around her and patted him on the back.

"As you all know by now," Coach Briggs continued, "three Kennedy High football players were caught on the Leesburg campus at three-twenty A.M. just as they finished dumping several bags of trash across the Leesburg commons.

"According to court records from this morning's hearing," he went on, "John Marquette, Ed Owens, and Bernie Hays will be on court probation for one month, reporting regularly to a parole officer. If you've noticed that they are not in school today, it's because the court also ordered that they spend whatever time was necessary to return the Leesburg campus to the condition they found it, and that's what they're doing right now."

Loud cheers and gasps went up from everyone on the mall, and several people clapped, showing their approval of this punishment.

"Nobody likes to lose," Coach Briggs went on. "But somebody has to, and Friday night it was our turn. There's no excuse for what happened after the game. The guilty parties deserve to be punished." He cleared his throat again. "The administration and the other coaches and I have decided that the boys will also be benched for next Friday night's game. This is going to be tough on us, because it means we'll be without four key players in that game, but we feel this is a goodwill gesture we need to make to Leesburg to impress upon them how sorry we are about what happened. That's all I have to say. Thank you for listening."

"And that's the latest news," Peter said soberly. "Thanks, Coach. Now back to music. Here's a new release that's sure to zoom up the charts — 'Baby BeeBop Mine' by the Moondrops."

As the music blared over the loudspeaker, the students on the quad gradually began to move around and talk. Chris and Greg walked by and waved. Fiona asked who they were and Diana told her. "And them?" she asked, pointing at Phoebe and Michael, "do they go together?"

"Yes," Diana said. "That's Phoebe and Michael. She's a childhood friend of Holly's." Diana smiled at Holly, trying to bring her into the conversation.

"How lovely!" Fiona said. "I already miss my friends in London."

"Oh, but you're really going to like it here," Diana said quickly. "You'll find everyone real easy to get to know."

Laurie Bennington walked up to them, a self-assured look on her face. "Hi, everyone," she smiled. Laurie had on black raw silk pants and a baggy black-and-white sweater with abstract designs on it. As usual, she looked cool and elegant, her hennaed hair swept back on one side and held with a handmade ceramic barrette that had a design similar to the sweater's.

"This must be Fiona!" Laurie said loudly. "I understand you're a dancer," she said, shaking

Fiona's hand. "I happen to know a lot about dance. We always go to all the performances at the Kennedy Center, and I studied dance for several years with Madame LaFrenière. That wouldn't mean much to very many people here," she said, glancing around the mall, "but I'm sure you know who she is."

Fiona looked impressed. "Of course! My mother teaches ballet professionally and is considering opening her own school in the city. Perhaps you could introduce her to Madame LaFrenière."

Laurie looked momentarily uncomfortable, but recovered quickly. "Well, I'll have to see. We didn't exactly part on the best of terms. We had a few personality clashes, I guess you could say. But my father has lots of contacts in the city — he's head of a cable station here — and I'm sure he could help arrange some introductions for you. Why don't you come with me and I'll show you the dance studio in the school?"

"That was nice of Laurie," Diana said as Fiona and Laurie left. "Well, I gotta go." She stood up. "See you in math tomorrow, Holly. See *you* at home tonight, whizzo," she said to Bart.

Ted had come over to talk to Bart. "Brentwood hasn't won a game against us in ten years," he said mournfully. "We had definite plans to keep it that way. Now it may be a more-than-even match Friday night."

Bart looked miserable. "I wish so much this hadn't happened," he said, touching his sling.

Ted looked at him curiously. "What is the real story on that injury, Einerson? I heard a couple of the guys saying Marquette purposely jumped on you when he saw you open. What do you think?"

"I didn't see what happened," Bart said firmly.

Ted shrugged. "If I were you, I'd say something to the coach."

Bart's silence was Ted's answer. The first bell sounded for fifth period classes and Holly got up. "Short lunch break on Mondays," she said. "I have to go."

Bart flashed his broadest grin at her. "See you soon!"

As Holly walked away, she saw Heather coming out of the building, heading straight for Bart.

Chapter 15

Holly and Bart walked out of the massive Department of Energy building on Washington Mall and sat down on a bench facing Independence Avenue, a long street that ran from the Washington Monument to the Capitol Building. Across from them was the imposing structure of the Smithsonian Institution, its dark, Russian-like architecture providing a startling contrast to the sweeping modern lines of the Department of Energy, and the elegance of the Capitol.

"That's got to be the biggest building I've ever been in," Bart said, shaking his head in awe as he looked back at the Department of Energy. "I don't know how anybody finds their way around. The only building I can think of that's bigger is the Pentagon — and a lot of the employees there actually carry maps with them."

Holly laughed. "I wouldn't want to work in either place. I like to feel a little more at home where I work. But I thought Mr. Everett was interesting, didn't you?"

"He seems incredibly conscientious," Bart agreed. "He gave us some great information for the report. How do you think you'll write yours?"

Holly smoothed the skirt of her lavender sweater dress and leaned back on her elbows, her face to the sun. "I don't know," she said lazily. "Maybe I'll write it like a question-and-answer interview."

"That's a great idea. Wish I'd thought of it first."

"I was also thinking about writing it as a personal reflection. Starting off talking about what I thought before I went into the interview, what I learned, and then how it changed my thinking. You know, sort of a personal essay."

"Hmmm. That sounds better than a straight report, too," Bart said, twisting to look at her. "Ouch!" He straightened up, a look of pain on his face. "Sometimes I forget about this shoulder. I guess that's a sign it's healing."

She smiled. "Dr. E. was certainly pleased with your X ray today."

"Yeah. He said everything is right on schedule and I should only have to wear this sling one more week."

"Good! Then it'll be your turn to drive," Holly teased. Her gaze wandered across the mall to the sculpture gardens that were part of the Smithsonian. She had visited them once before. When her father had been in town on business last year, she had taken the bus from Baltimore into downtown Washington, D.C., and they had spent a day touring the Capitol, going to the top of the Washington Monument, and seeing as much as possible of the Air and Space Museum. At the end of the day they had taken a brief walk through the beautiful gardens.

"Bart," she said suddenly, "have you seen the Smithsonian Gardens? Let's walk through them. It won't take long, and since you can't go to football practice. . . ." As soon as Holly said this, she blushed, amazed by her own forwardness.

But Bart agreed immediately, and several minutes later they had crossed the busy street and were strolling through the gardens, admiring all the flowers still in bloom and the layout of the formal areas. Holly was surprised by how much Bart knew about the plants until he reminded her that he had grown up on a ranch and spent almost all his time outdoors.

"You should see the ranch, Holly. To an Easterner, things might look pretty brown most of the time, but once you get to know the land, you see how much grows there and how much it changes all year round." Bart had a faraway look in his eyes.

"You miss it a lot, don't you?"

He smiled. "I do miss it. You can't imagine how beautiful it is there. We're going back for Christmas. I can hardly wait to ride my horse again. In the evenings, when the weather's nice, we sit out on the porch and watch the sunset and sometimes I play my guitar. The TV reception isn't very good, so we aren't even tempted by that. The nights are so magical there."

Bart reached out with his right hand and took

her left hand, sending shivers through her. She smiled at him, and they walked hand-in-hand in silence for several minutes. When Bart was reflective like this, she found him irresistible. He dropped the mask of brashness and was just himself — a likeable, easygoing person with lots of interests who could talk about anything. She loved hearing about the family ranch in Montana. She saw a whole different side to him when he talked about it — a deep, emotional side.

"Holly — " Bart said hesitantly, pausing next to an especially beautiful display of rose bushes, "would you go to the costume party with me Saturday night?"

She felt her cheeks redden, but looked directly into his eyes and said, "I'd like that, Bart."

"What about the guy from the clinic you date?" he asked, looking as though he could hardly believe her answer.

"What about him?"

"You know what I mean. Aren't you seeing him?"

"As a matter of fact, I'm not," Holly answered. "He's just a friend."

"Really?" Bart's face lit up in a broad smile.

"Really."

"Holly — " Bart glanced around. For the moment, they were alone. He reached up and gently touched her cheek with his fingers. Then, placing his hand on the back of her head, he lowered his face toward hers and kissed her. Her head was swimming. She kissed him back and wished that it would never stop. She wanted to melt into his arms, so sweet was his kiss. As she pressed her body closer to his, she felt him draw back from her. Startled, she pulled away, too. The kiss had ended much too soon. Then Holly noticed that two people had appeared on the path behind them, and she and Bart started walking again, a comfortable silence between them. He held her hand tightly and gave it a squeeze.

"Have you decided on a costume for the party?" he asked as they strolled along a narrow path with lush flowers on either side.

"Girls are at a disadvantage. Male characters outnumber female characters about ten to one."

"Does that mean you're dressing up as a male character?" he teased.

"No. It just means I don't have as many choices as you. I'm going as Catherine Barkley."

Bart looked at her blankly. "Who?"

"The English nurse from Ernest Hemingway's novel *A Farewell to Arms*."

Bart shook his head. "I haven't read it. Is she like Florence Nightingale?"

"Not quite as heroic," Holly laughed. "But she is a nurse on the war front, and she has this torrid love affair, and then she dies."

"Sounds great," Bart said dubiously. "But I suppose you chose her because she's a nurse."

"Right. I didn't have too many choices. So what cowboy are you going as?"

Bart chuckled. "It's that obvious, huh? As a matter of fact, I *am* going as a cowboy of sorts. Shane."

"Perfect!" Holly exclaimed. "That's about as obvious as me being a nurse. Do you have your costume?"

117

"Most of it. I still need chaps and a buckskin shirt, but I have everything else."

They continued their walk, talking quietly, sharing their thoughts on school, the upcoming party, and the future prospects of the football team. Holly told Bart a little bit about Steven, but all she said about her date with him was that he wasn't very tolerant of other people, and she had found it hard to talk to him because they frequently disagreed. "I'd still like to be friends with him, though."

"You think you can be friends with someone you're not dating anymore?" Bart asked, surprised.

"Sure, why not?"

"I guess after I quit dating a girl, that's it. We don't stay friends. But maybe I never tried."

"My mom and dad are pretty good friends, and that's in spite of a divorce," Holly said. "I know a lot of it is for my sake, but I think they'd be friends anyway. My mom isn't crazy about my stepmother, but she's even learning to get along with her now."

"You seem to accept your parents' divorce pretty well."

She shrugged. "What option do I have?"

He stopped by a bench and motioned for her to sit down beside him. "I probably shouldn't talk about this," he said slowly, "because if it ever got out, it would be bad for my dad's political career, so none of us talk about it. That's the problem." He stared at the ground. Holly waited silently. "My parents are having some problems, too," Bart said at last, his words coming in a rush. "Mom isn't happy here in Washington. She'd like to go back to Montana. But Dad's career is here now. So I worry about that. And right now I'm supposed to be making decisions like where to go to college and what to be. It's getting to be too much." His voice was tight.

Holly searched for the right thing to say. She wished she could put her arms around him and assure him that everything would be okay. But how could she be sure that was true? Instead she took his hand in both of hers and gently stroked it. Bart continued to talk, opening up more and more, telling her about his indecision, his concerns, and his longings for home.

"My mother thinks I don't have any problems. My sister wants to tell me her problems but since she kind of looks up to me, I don't feel like burdening her with my own. My dad wants me to go to an Ivy League college and then to law school. He's never even asked me what I really want to do. I guess he doesn't want to hear what I'm going to say. Inside I sometimes feel like I'm coming apart. I'm afraid my parents might decide to get divorced and that I'll end up in a dead-end career that I hate instead of back on the ranch where I want to be. I just feel all this pressure building up and I can't seem to tell my folks about it. I never see my dad much anyway."

Bart stopped and turned away from Holly. When she started talking, her voice was so soft, he had to turn toward her to hear her.

"My parents were divorced when I was eleven, and for a long time I thought if I was very, very good and did everything everybody wanted me to do, Daddy would come home and we would all be happy again. So I tried. I really did. I got good grades in school, and kept my room neat, and never talked back to my mother — you name it, I did it. And Daddy still didn't come home. So then I did just the opposite. I made threats and misbehaved and I made sure my mother knew that my unhappiness was all her fault. But that didn't bring Daddy home, either."

Now Bart took Holly's hand, and stroked it, his touch sending shivers up her spine. His eyes were wide and full of compassion as he listened. "So what happened?" he asked when she paused. "How did you — "

"Learn to accept it?" she said, finishing his thought for him. "Well, I finally realized that what had happened to them had nothing to do with me. I was sort of an innocent bystander. I didn't like not having both of them with me, and I hated to see my mother so unhappy — and she was for a long time — but I finally realized I couldn't do anything about it. I couldn't change the divorce. They did what they had to do for themselves. I didn't have to accept any responsibility for that. And Bart," she said, looking directly into his clear blue eyes, "neither do you. If it happens, you'll make the best of it. But you can't stop it from happening if it's going to, so it will only add to your pressure if you worry about it. You've got your own problems. What's happening to your parents can't be one of them. Right now you need to concentrate on picking a college and a career. And if your parents divorce — and based on what you've said, they might not even be thinking about it — but if they do, then that's just the way it is. Life goes on."

Very slowly, Bart circled his good arm around her and hugged her. "How did you get so smart?" he asked, smiling at her.

Touched by his words, Holly felt her eyes mist over and a lump sprang up in her throat. "It's just common sense," she whispered. "You're carrying around an unnecessary burden. Let it go."

"I think it's gone," he whispered back. "I think you dissolved it. You should become a psychologist instead of a nurse."

He kissed her again, and again Holly responded with passion. No one had ever kissed her like this before. It felt so good, so right. They sat huddled together on the bench, Holly nestling her head against Bart's good shoulder. "Anyway, I can't be a psychologist," she said, picking up the conversation where it had left off. "I like medicine too much."

"Then be a doctor."

"What?"

Bart sat up straight and said earnestly, "Be a doctor. Why a nurse? Why not be a doctor? That way, you're the one calling the shots instead of the one taking the orders."

"I've never even thought of it."

"You should," Bart said, excited.

"It would be so expensive, and all those years of school."

"There are ways to finance your own education," Bart said firmly. "In Montana we have a program through our state university that helps qualified students through medical school if they'll practice in rural areas when they finish."

"Rural?"

"Like where I live. Out in the wide open spaces, far from town. It's hard to get good doctors in such isolated areas."

Holly was intrigued. "I would love to be a doctor, but . . . but . . . well, I guess I have a lot to think about."

He turned to her, his blue eyes twinkling. "Hey, I like the idea of you coming to practice in Montana." He bent toward her again, and gave her one more kiss.

They looked at each other and reluctantly stood up to leave, then walked slowly back to Holly's car, tightly holding hands. The silence between them was a comfortable, natural peace. Holly had never felt so wonderful in her life. This is it, she thought in awe. I'm falling in love.

Only the tiniest fear tugged at her thoughts as she walked along, but for just this once, Holly refused to acknowledge it.

Chapter
16

Holly waited for Phoebe on the front steps of the high school. It was a warm Friday afternoon. The Indian summer weather had continued and the forecast was for a beautiful weekend. Around her, the huge trees that shaded the high school campus were dressed in brilliant shades of red, yellow, gold, and orange.

But while nature was in its glory, the spirit of the student body at Kennedy High School was subdued. It was a sharp contrast to just one week ago when everyone had been so excited about Kennedy's game with Leesburg. Tonight they would play Brentwood, a team that had not won a game against them in ten years, and everyone predicted that with four starting players out of the Kennedy lineup, Brentwood could count on taking home a victory.

The pep squad had decorated the halls for the game, but nothing looked as festive as it had last week. No spontaneous cheers filled the hallways. Everyone said out loud that Kennedy would win the game, but nobody really believed it.

"Hi, Holly!" Phoebe came running down the steps, her red hair flying behind her, her blue cub scout shirt flapping in the breeze.

She stopped and caught her breath. "It's a perfect day to take a walk through the park. I ordered this incredible weather just for us."

"Nice trick," laughed Holly. "Teach me how to do it sometime, will you?"

They crossed several busy streets, then entered the park. Dry leaves crunched under their feet. Ahead of them a man and woman walked, their arms wrapped around each other.

Phoebe smiled at Holly. "Too bad you have to work tonight and miss the game again. But I doubt it will be as exciting as last week's game."

"I wish I could go anyway," Holly said, "but I'd rather skip the game than your party."

"Then you're coming for sure? You won't have to work?"

Holly rolled her eyes. "I better not. They know at the clinic that I'm going to a party. Have you got your costume?"

"I'll be finishing it up tomorrow *and* helping Sasha and Kim get everything ready at the bookstore." Phoebe groaned. "But I'll have most of the day to work on my costume because we can't get into the bookstore to decorate until it closes at five o'clock. Michael and I are going over to Janie's in the morning. She's going to do a little bit of sewing for us. Everybody's been asking her, but she doesn't seem to mind. She's got this great room in her basement where her machine is all set up."

"Who are you going as?"

"I'll tell if you will," Phoebe teased. "I'm going as Pippi Longstocking."

"Fantastic, Pheeb!" laughed Holly. "You've already got the right hair color and the mischievous grin. Pippi's a great character. I read every one of the books."

Holly told her about Catherine Barkley. "The nurse's uniform is easy, and a friend of Mom's has this real authentic-looking bright blue cape I borrowed, but you wouldn't believe how much trouble I had getting a nurse's hat. I finally found one at a nursing supply house in Arlington. I'm going to pick it up in the morning. Nurses just don't wear hats anymore," Holly said.

"You make me want to reread *A Farewell to Arms*," Phoebe sighed. "I think I've read it twice already. I always cry when Catherine dies, it's *so* sad." She pulled a bright red leaf from the branch of a tree they were passing. "Are you coming to the party with anybody?"

"As a matter of fact, I am." Holly smiled.

"With Bart?" Phoebe asked expectantly. "Really?" she said excitedly when Holly nodded. "He's crazy about you, Holly. I was watching him look at you during lunch today. You two make a perfect couple."

Holly's pretty face clouded over. "I like him better than any boy I've ever known, Pheeb, but. . . ."

"But what?"

"He — he flirts with other girls so much. I can't ask him to stop because I haven't even had a real date with him yet."

"You couldn't possibly be thinking about Heather Richardson, could you?"

"It's mostly her, but he does it with lots of girls. Sometimes when I'm with him, I just want to fade away. When we're alone, he's wonderful. The problem is at school when other girls are around."

"So tell him what's bugging you."

She sighed. "I tried once, but I just couldn't think of any tactful way to do it without sounding jealous and pushy. Other than that," she said, glancing up at her old friend, "everything's fantastic." She smiled shyly. "I think I'm in love for the first time in my life, and suddenly *everything* seems special."

"I know what you mean." Phoebe nodded. "You feel like you can do anything, you're so happy all the time. Love is the most special feeling in the world."

"What are you going to do if you and Michael go to different colleges next year?"

Phoebe sat down in a pile of leaves and began to bury her legs in them. "Like I said the other day, we'll just make the best of it and we'll both try to come home whenever we can so we can see each other. We both know it's important to get the best education we can. I think I understand why everybody looks back on high school with nostalgia. It's the last easy time of your life. After that, you have to take lots of responsibility and start making decisions," she said wistfully. "I guess I'd better resolve right now to enjoy the rest of my senior year as much as I can."

She stood up and they continued their walk. "What's happening with your mother and her boyfriend?" Phoebe asked Holly.

"Mom thinks he's going to propose soon. She's so funny about it — one minute she wants him to and the next minute she doesn't. But I'm pretty sure if he doesn't hurry up and do it, she'll do it for him." Holly giggled. "She's already hinting at a June wedding."

"You seem happy about it."

"I am. It'll be a big adjustment having Bruce live with us, but he and Mom are really in love and it's great seeing her so happy."

"Just like you."

Holly smiled. "Just like me."

At five o'clock on Saturday Holly had her costume completed and was taking a shower so she could start getting ready for the party. Even though she wasn't picking up Bart until eight, she wanted to make sure everything was perfect — her hair, her makeup, and her costume.

Work had gone well the previous night. During a slow period, she and Dr. Ellerbee had time to talk and Holly had asked him how difficult it was for students with very little money to get through medical school. He had given her a quizzical look.

"Are you asking that for yourself, Holly?"

"Yes," she confessed hesitantly.

"Good!" He smiled. "I think you'd make an excellent doctor!"

127

She had beamed when he said that. Now that the idea of being a doctor was taking root, she was growing more and more excited about the possibility. "But money's going to be a problem for me," she told him.

"There are ways to do it," he said encouragingly. "You should talk to Steven Ewing about it. He's going to be putting himself through medical school and he probably knows every method of financing available."

Holly had promised she would the next time they were both working. "I'm pleased that you're thinking about this," Dr. Ellerbee had said. "Being a doctor is a difficult, demanding career and it takes a special person to succeed. From what I've observed in the time you've worked for us, you have the right qualities."

Holly was anxious to share this conversation with Bart. She had talked to him on the phone at noon, but decided to wait until tonight to tell him about it. Bart had his costume and last night's game on his mind.

"I wish you could have been there, Holly. Even though we lost, our team played well. Ted nearly saved it for us! If he'd had some strong blockers, he would have made that touchdown in the fourth quarter and we would have won."

"You're right," Holly had said. "Look at the score — thirteen to twelve. That's nothing to be ashamed of."

"The best moment was when the crowd gave us a standing ovation at the end of the game. The whole team was really moved by that. I can't wait until I'm back in action. Just two more weeks!"

"It could be three or four," Holly said gently. "Your injury needs time to heal completely or else — "

"Okay, okay, *Dr.* Daniels," Bart had laughed.

He told her he had found the chaps he needed to complete his outfit and they had chatted for several more minutes before hanging up.

As Holly showered, she found herself singing. Everything was so wonderful! Her mother's happiness, thoughts about being a doctor, and most of all, Bart. He had promised her that as soon as the sling was off his arm, he would play his guitar for her. He was starting to make *future* plans with her. Not very far in the future — just a week or two — but anytime a boy had done that in the past, she had felt panicky. Everything was so different with Bart.

As she stepped out of the shower, she heard the phone ring. She waited for her mother to pick it up, but it continued to ring. She must have gone out for a few minutes. Wrapped in a towel, Holly went out to the hallway to answer it.

"Holly, it's Dr. Ellerbee," said the deep voice at the other end. A wave of panic swept through her. No! He couldn't do this to her! She *absolutely would not* work. She was going to a party, with Bart. *Nothing* was more important than that.

"I hate to ask, Holly, but once again I'm at your mercy," he said. "Remember the accident victim who died at the clinic earlier this week? I have to attend a coroner's hearing at the hospital this evening, and Steven will be the only aide on duty. He'll need help. Dr. Myers is filling in for me. I've called all the other aides, and I can't come up with a single one who can work. It will only be from six to nine. I know you have a party tonight, so I promise not to get back late."

Holly felt like crying. Her first real date with Bart, and she would be an hour late. Not only that, but she'd have to get ready in a hurry. *And* she would be working with Steven for the first time since their date. What a rotten break.

"Holly?"

She bit her lip and pushed down the lump in her throat. "I'm here, Dr. E. If you'll promise that it's just until nine, then — okay."

"I appreciate this, Holly. You're a true professional. I have some new thoughts for you about financing medical school, and perhaps your undergraduate education as well."

"Thanks, Dr. E. I'll see you at six," she said.

She called Bart and told him what had happened. He was very understanding. "So I'll pick you up a little bit after nine," she said.

"You'll get to the party a lot sooner if you don't have to come over here first. I'll catch a ride with Ted and you can come straight to the party from work. That makes a lot more sense," he said.

"Yes. I suppose so," she agreed, trying to hide her disappointment.

"At least you're wearing a nurse's costume. If you were coming as some sort of monster, you might cause a couple of coronaries in the emergency room tonight," Bart joked.

She smiled in spite of herself as she hung up. Bart could be so sweet. And probably what was upsetting her was that she wasn't going to have the satisfaction of arriving at the party with him — something she had looked forward to because it would show everybody in the crowd that the two of them were now a couple. "That's silly," she said to herself. "Bart will be waiting for me — and that's all that matters."

"Hi ya, Holly-dolly," Steven said as she came into the clinic office two hours later.

"Hi," she said simply, quickly moving over to the locker area and putting her costume away in it.

"So tonight's the big costume party, huh? And you're probably going as Florence Nightingale, right?"

"Wrong. Catherine Barkley."

"Ah, good old Hemingway," Steven said immediately. *"A Farewell to Arms.* One of my favorites."

"Really?" Holly was impressed. She had never thought of Steven as a reader.

"And do you have a date?"

"Yes."

"Anybody I know?" Steven's voice sounded friendly.

"You met him last Friday night. He was in here for a shoulder separation," she said self-consciously.

"I remember." Steven nodded. "Superjock. One of your awesome athletic friends from Kennedy High, right?"

Holly glared at him. "Right," she mumbled, angered by the tone in Steven's voice.

"Don't get mad." Steven smiled. "I was just teasing. Actually he seemed like a nice kid."

Holly sighed. She turned to face him. "His name is Bart and he's not the kind of person you think he is. He's very nice."

"Did I say he wasn't?" Steven asked defensively. "I didn't say two words. I just thought maybe you and I — "

She smiled at him but shook her head. "I don't think so, Steven. I like you a lot, but you and I are just too different. We think differently about things. Let's just keep working together as friends, okay?"

Steven studied her a moment without saying anything. "Okay. Friends." He took her hand and shook it.

She smiled again. "So listen, friend," she said, giving him a poke in the ribs, "I'm under doctor's orders — Dr. Ellerbee's orders — to talk to you about financing medical school. Dr. E. says you know all about it, and I'm thinking seriously of setting my sights on being a doctor."

"Smart move, Daniels," Steven said approvingly. "I think you could pull it off."

Chapter 17

"Who was on the phone?" Diana asked, coming into the kitchen.

"Holly," Bart said, tasting the soup he was stirring on the stove. "She has to work for a few hours and is going to meet me at the party. I told her I would get a ride with Ted." He glanced up as Diana walked over to him, and burst out laughing.

"That's great! I love it!" he gasped between chuckles. "If Jeremy really looks like your identical twin, you two will win every prize they give tonight."

"Thank you very much," Diana said in a voice like one of the munchkins in *The Wizard of Oz*. She shuffled around the kitchen, her knees locked together and her feet angled away from each other. Bart howled in laughter.

Diana's trip to the thrift shop had resulted in her wearing a pair of khaki pants that had last been worn by a very fat man. Her striped knit shirt also had once belonged to a heavy person. She had tied a huge feather pillow around her waist, to make a very round, fat stomach. The pointed collar on her shirt had "Dum" stitched on one side and a bright red bow was tied under her chin. She wore a child's gold-and-blue beanie, and she had made up her face with lots of black freckles. She really looked like she had stepped from the pages of *Through the Looking Glass*, where Alice meets the absurd twins who always finish each other's thoughts and cry "Ditto! Ditto!"

Bart's hard work had also paid off. He wore a light-colored fringed buckskin shirt, jeans with chaps over them, a Western bandanna, and his cowboy boots and spurs. His Stetson hat lay on the counter. His mother had sewed leather fringe onto his sling.

He carefully poured two cups of soup and set them on the counter. Diana hopped up on a stool and began to sip hers. "You're getting pretty handy working with just one arm," she said with admiration.

Her compliment pleased Bart and he acknowledged it with a bow. "I'll be looking forward to having both arms, though. This is a drag. Did Mom and Dad get to see your costume before they left for their party?"

Diana nodded. "Boy, did they laugh! Mom actually had tears in her eyes. She kept talking about when she used to read the Alice stories to us when we were little kids. You make a pretty handsome Shane, Bart. It's a good thing the movie's already been made. Alan Ladd would have had some strong competition for the lead!"

He winked at her, assuming his most macho air. " 'A man's gotta do what a man's gotta do.' " he said in a deep voice, reciting the most famous line from the book. "My sling just adds authenticity — makes me look like I had a gunfight down at the OK Corral."

"Whatever you say," Diana replied. She picked up a copy of Friday's *The Red and the Gold* from the counter. "What did you think about the editorial Sasha Jenkins wrote in yesterday's paper?"

"I thought she did a good job of saying some things that needed to be said."

"Me, too," Diana agreed. "I especially liked this part." She began to read aloud. " 'There's never a valid excuse for destroying the property of others. Pranks are common among high school students, but there's a clearly defined line between innocent fun and malicious intent. Last Friday night, that line was crossed. While the lawns at Leesburg Military Academy will recover, we hope the guilty parties will always remember their humiliation in having to clean them up.' I wonder if John Marquette has seen this."

"He wasn't in school yesterday, but I'll bet somebody told him about it. I sure hope he doesn't get mad and take it out on Sasha. You and I found out last month when we were making the video that he can be a bad sport," Bart said.

Diana slowly sipped her soup. "Do you think he feels bad about Kennedy High losing last night?"

"I'll bet he does," Bart said. "John's a good

player. He probably knows that if he'd been playing he might have made a difference."

"You, too."

"Me, too," Bart sighed. Watching his teammates fight so hard, only to lose by one point, had been painful for him. He was far more frustrated by his shoulder injury than he was letting on to anybody, with the possible exception of Holly, who instinctively understood. He had never been the kind of athlete who could tolerate sitting on the bench during a game. When he played he gave his best, and usually that was good enough for him to make the first team.

"Bart, did John purposely jump you?"

He frowned. He had been asked this several times now and had dodged the question. But he couldn't do that with Diana. "I'll never know," he said. "He didn't have any reason to."

"He's jealous of you because all the girls like you. And he's still angry at me for dumping him and going out with Jeremy."

"We can't worry about it, Di. Let's give him the benefit of the doubt."

"That sounds just like you. Always the peacemaker." She smiled at him. "Mom and Dad seemed awfully happy tonight. Ever since you were injured, they've been spending a lot of time together. Have you noticed?"

"Maybe," he said cautiously. "But parents probably always pull together when one of their kids is sick or injured. I don't know that it means anything."

He saw her bite her lip and blink back tears. "Look," he said gently, "Mom and Dad have got to work out whatever problems they're having. We can't do that for them. They want things to work out, and they're trying hard. I have a lot of faith in them and I know you do, too."

"But we can — "

"No, we can't," he said softly.

"We — "

"No."

"What if they. . . ."

"Decide on a divorce?" He looked at her intently. "I've been thinking about it a lot lately. Just look around you at all the kids you know whose parents are divorced. They make the best of it. Otherwise, everybody's miserable, and what's the point of that?"

She looked at him suspiciously. "Where did all this newfound wisdom come from? I've never heard you talk like this before."

Bart smiled, a vision of Holly before him. "Let's just say a friend helped me to understand a few things. A smart friend."

"Well, I have to admit what you're saying makes sense," Diana said slowly, wiping a tear from her eye, "but I still want them to stay together more than anything. . . . Only I know you're right — it doesn't hang on what you and I do or don't do. I guess I've been pretty silly about that."

They ate in silence for a minute. Bart felt Diana looking at him and glanced at her. "What is it?" he asked.

She hesitated. "Bart, what's been bothering you lately?"

He looked startled. "Nothing. Why?"

"Something has been. Both Mom and I have noticed. Something other than your arm because it started before that. Even Dad said something about it."

Bart studied the bottom of his soup cup, hesitant to share his concerns. He didn't want Diana worrying about him. He knew her too well. If he told her he had a problem, it would instantly become her problem. She had always been that way, and it was a quality that was both endearing and irritating because she would try to find a solution for him. That's how she had approached their parents' problems — thinking that if she and Bart were happy, that would somehow solve everything for them.

"I'm trying to come to grips with lots of things," he said after a moment, picking his words with care. "What's happening with the folks, and where to go to college and what career to plan for, stuff like that."

"You'll probably go back to Montana, won't you?"

Bart looked at her in surprise. "Dad expects me to go to an Eastern university and be a lawyer."

"What makes you think that?"

"Well, he's all but said so."

Diana looked at him intently. "Bart, you dope. That's not the same as *actually* saying so. Dad's proud of Montana. I think you'd better sit down and talk to him instead of assuming you know what he's thinking. I have a feeling he'd be pleased to find out you want to stay on the ranch."

Bart eyed her with doubt. "Really?"

"Really!"

He put his good arm around Diana and hugged her hard. "Ouch!" she squealed. "You want Tweedledum going to the party with bruises?" But she started to laugh.

"You're right. I really should talk to Dad. I'm going to say something to him tomorrow. C'mon, let's get the kitchen cleaned up. It's time to party!"

"First you have to tell me."

"Tell you what?"

"Who your smart friend is."

"See if you can guess."

"Holly."

"How'd you guess so quick?"

"I'm not *stupid*. It was the look on your face when you were talking about your 'friend.' " Diana grinned at him. "You really like her, don't you?"

"Yeah. I really do." He smiled broadly.

"Usually when I say that about a girl you're dating, you deny that you like her. Holly must be different."

Bart shrugged. "Maybe." Then he laughed. "Okay, I confess that she's different. She's more mature than other girls I know. She doesn't play silly games. And in case you haven't noticed, she's very beautiful."

"Have you told her how you feel?"

Bart's cheeks reddened. "Well, no. Not yet. I mean, we hardly know each other. But maybe tonight I will."

Diana laughed and gave him a gentle punch in the ribs. "I think you should. She shouldn't be the last one to know something like that."

Bart sighed happily. "I have a feeling this is going to be something special. I can't wait to see her tonight."

Chapter 18

"Sasha," Phoebe called out. "Hello! Where are you?" She shut the back door of the Albatross behind her, using her foot to nudge it closed. She was carrying two heavy grocery sacks filled with large bottles of soda. She carefully set them down on a table in the back office of the bookstore.

"Whew!" she gasped, out of breath. "I think I need to start working out with weights or something to build some upper body strength. The real Pippi Longstocking wouldn't have any trouble carrying these. She's famous for her strength. Sasha, where are you?"

"I'm here," Sasha called from the other room. "Come see!"

Phoebe walked into the main room of the bookstore, her eyes shining with excitement as she looked around. "Everything looks fabulous! Wow!"

141

Sasha was standing on a stepstool, retaping several orange-and-black crepe-paper streamers to a ceiling light fixture. The small cozy bookstore with its high bookcases and dark wood had been transformed into a Halloween party room with decorations and streamers covering almost every surface. The sales counter had been reserved for refreshments and had been pushed against the front window to make space for a small dance floor.

"I love your costume!" Sasha said, looking at Phoebe and laughing. "You really look like Pippi Longstocking." Phoebe was wearing a ragged shirt covered with colorful patches. It went to her knees and under it were cotton pantyhose with one green leg and one brown leg. She was also wearing a huge pair of men's shoes. She had used spray-in coloring to make her hair even redder than usual and had it braided and tied with colorful bits of rags. She had used a makeup pencil to cover her face with freckles. She had also created a gap between her front teeth with special makeup so that she looked like impish little Pippi. Now if only I were as tall as Pippi, Phoebe thought ruefully.

"Michael's coming as Robin Hood," Phoebe said. "His mother made him a bright green tunic and hat and he got some men's tights the same color at the theatrical supply house in Georgetown. He's going to be wearing his little brother's bow and arrow set. I can't wait to see him!"

She fixed a streamer that was drooping along the edge of one of the book display cases. "What made you and Rob decide to come as

Daisy and Jay Gatsby, Sasha?"

"*The Great Gatsby*'s a favorite book for both of us. And besides, Rob has a friend who has a white suit that would be perfect for Gatsby. So that made it easy. And you know how much I love flapper dresses. I had a lot of fun getting my costume together and finding the right jewelry."

Phoebe smiled at her. "Kim ought to be getting here any minute. Don't you want to go get dressed, Sasha? The party starts in less than two hours!"

Sasha climbed down from the stool and began gathering up scissors, tape, a hammer, and nails. "I think that finishes the decorations. Did you get the other stuff?"

Phoebe nodded. "It's in my car. While you get dressed, I'll get everything else set out and make sure the tape deck is all ready. I'm glad we decided not to try apple bobbing. Your folks were right — it's too much of a mess for here."

"Everybody will probably be expecting a haunted house, too, but no room for that, either. Maybe having a party here wasn't such a good idea," Sasha said, looking around anxiously.

"Hey, it's a *perfect* place," Phoebe said. "Besides, this is meant to be a costume party and a dance. We don't need those other things." She paused, listening. "I think I hear Kim."

"Hi!" Kim said, coming in the back way. She was dressed as Antigone. Her toga was a white sheet trimmed with gold brocade that swished around her feet. She was carrying a box filled with snacks from Earthly Delights that she and

143

her mother had made for the party. "Looks nice," she said unenthusiastically, looking around.

"What's the matter?" asked Phoebe as she began helping Kim get the food out. "You sound upset."

"I am. I'm mad at my mom."

"How come?" asked Sasha, nibbling on a large mushroom stuffed with feta cheese. "Mmmm! This is delicious! Think your mom would give me the recipe?"

"You'll have to ask her yourself," Kim said. "I don't plan to speak to her for a while."

"What happened?" Phoebe asked, concerned. Kim and her mother had one of the best relationships she knew of. She had never seen Kim so angry.

"You know how anxious Mom is to cater some of the big parties given by government officials," Kim said as she took out a tray of tiny croissants and began to arrange them. "Well, last night she catered a dinner at the Richardsons'."

"Heather's parents?" asked Sasha and Phoebe together.

Kim nodded. "Well, Mrs. Richardson told my mother that her darling Heather had her heart set on going to our party, and that I was one of the hostesses. I guess she was pretty upset that she wasn't invited. Mrs. Richardson knew that my mom would feel obligated to invite Heather herself."

"Well, now we know where Heather gets her personality," Phoebe commented.

"So my mother went ahead and said, 'Oh, I'm sure the girls would love for Heather to come,'"

Kim continued. " 'I'll just invite her for them.' Then Heather came into the kitchen, and my mother told her, too, so Heather *and* one of her girl friends are coming tonight. My own mother invited them! Can you believe that?"

Kim looked so upset that Phoebe and Sasha rushed to assure her that it was okay with them and not to worry about it. "I don't really care that she's coming," Kim said, close to tears. "But Holly and Bart are coming together tonight and I just know Heather will do some dumb thing that will upset Holly and it'll be my fault."

"Don't worry about it, Kim. We'll all try to keep Heather away from Bart," Phoebe tried to reassure her. "But if something does happen, it won't have anything to do with you."

Kim sighed. "I'm really sorry. I can't understand why my mom would do such a thing, but I guess she was really put on the spot."

"Forget about it, Kim. Just relax and have a good time. The food looks fantastic — I can't wait to try one of the miniature cream puffs — and we'll all keep an eye on Heather. Sasha, let Kim and me finish up here while you get dressed," Phoebe said, carrying Kim's food box to the back.

"Hey, Sasha, that was a great editorial in the paper yesterday," Kim said, her voice softening. "You said what needed to be said."

"Thanks," Sasha replied, giving her a quick hug. "Now quit worrying about tonight. Everything's going to be fine."

Sasha left and Kim and Phoebe began putting out napkins and arranging the food.

Chapter *19*

The bookstore was jammed with costumed kids when Diana and Jeremy arrived. Fiona was with them, hovering shyly behind them, as though she was afraid of the noisy crowd.

As soon as they walked through the narrow front door, Diana and Jeremy locked elbows, silly grins on their faces. Everyone who noticed them burst into laughter at their Tweedledum and Tweedledee outfits and mannerisms. Diana had "Dum" embroidered on her collar, Jeremy had "Dee" on his. Even though Jeremy was taller than Diana, with their identical clothing, makeup, and silly grins, they looked like twins. When they talked in their munchkin voices, no one could keep from laughing.

Fiona smiled at their foolishness. She was dressed as Tinker Bell from *Peter Pan*, but had added white tights and pink satin ballet slippers to the flimsy, short-skirted outfit, showing off her long slender dancer's legs.

Woody, dressed as his favorite detective, Sherlock Holmes, came up to greet Fiona.

"Who's the girl in the low-cut velvet dress?" she asked curiously.

Woody followed her gaze, peering from beneath his Sherlock Holmes hat, his houndstooth-checked cape wrapped around him. Fiona was looking at Heather, who was not only dressed as Scarlett O'Hara from *Gone with the Wind*, but was acting the part by flirting outrageously with every boy there. She was wearing more makeup than usual and had her hair done in an elaborate antebellum style. One of her girl friends stood next to her, dressed as some kind of Indian maiden. As usual, the friend's role was to hover close to Heather, giggling at her jokes, and giving her someone to talk to when no boys were around.

As Woody was telling Fiona who Heather was, Ted joined them. He was dressed as Babe Ruth, his baseball hero and the main character of *The Babe Ruth Story*. His pockets were filled with miniature Baby Ruth candy bars, which he was handing out to everyone.

"You know what she asked me?" he said, when Woody made a comment about Heather.

Woody puffed on his unlit Sherlock Holmes pipe. "What?"

"She wanted to know if I thought Bart liked her."

"Bart? Isn't that the chap with his arm in a

sling?" asked Fiona. "Is he here? I haven't seen him."

"He's here and he's waiting for Holly to arrive. Phoebe's keeping an eye on him. One of us should dance with Heather to keep her away from Bart," he suggested, eyeing Ted.

"Hey, no way!" Ted protested. "I know I'm one of the few guys here without a date, but she is *not my type*. Bart can take care of himself."

Ted explained to Fiona what was going on and quickly asked her to dance.

Woody laughed. "I guess that leaves me with Heather, since Kim's so busy I can't even find her. Well," he took a deep breath. "Here goes." And he headed for Heather.

Diana watched Fiona dancing with Ted. She turned to Jeremy, accidentally bumping her pillow stomach into his. Jeremy took her hand affectionately. "I think Fiona is starting to like it here. I was afraid she would be a wallflower all night."

"She's doing great." Diana smiled. "And it's really a fun party. We should have one every year."

"Diana, Jeremy, I want you to meet my boyfriend Brad," Brenda said, coming up behind them, her face flushed with happiness.

Brad smiled. "Nice to meet you. Your outfits are terrific."

"Thank you very much," they replied together.

Brad and Brenda laughed. They were dressed as Caesar and Cleopatra. Brenda had on a black Egyptian-styled wig and a strapless gold lamé floor-length dress that hung very straight on her slim figure. She was wearing heavy gold jewelry and had put on exaggerated black eye makeup and bright red lipstick. Brad was wearing a toga with silver trim and had a laurel wreath around his forehead.

"You're pre-med at Princeton, aren't you?" Diana asked him. "I have a good friend who's interested in medical school. I know she'll want to talk to you when she gets here."

Janie, dressed like Becky Thatcher in a cotton calico dress, bloomers, and a sunbonnet, and Henry, dressed like Tom Sawyer, arrived just then. They came over to talk to Brad, whom they hadn't seen since August.

"Henry, you ought to be wearing the most elaborate costume here since you're a clothes designer, and look at you! Old, rolled-up overalls, a red bandanna around your neck, and a corncob pipe!" laughed Brenda. "Don't let Calvin Klein see you!"

"Ooh, look who just came in," Janie said. Laurie Bennington swept into the room. She was dressed entirely in deep purple, with a tight, long purple skirt and purple turtleneck. Over them she wore a sweeping purple cape and she had a crown on her head.

"Lady Macbeth, methinks," Janie said dryly. "Talk about type-casting. That's a perfect choice for her."

Laurie swept past them with a wave in their direction, Dick Westergard following behind her. He was dressed elaborately as the Count of Monte

Cristo and was wearing a brocade jacket, an elaborate ruffled shirt, knee-length pants, and white tights.

"Hi, everybody." He gestured to Laurie, who had gone over to the food table. "I'm accompanying Lady Macbeth tonight. I'm doing my best," he winked, "to stay out of the way of her dagger."

Peter Lacey, the reincarnation of Tarzan in a leopard loincloth, and Monica Ford, as a more sedate Jane, arrived with Chris and Greg.

"I can tell that Greg is supposed to be Captain Ahab from *Moby Dick* — the pegleg is a dead giveaway — but what about Chris?" asked Jeremy.

"Anna Karenina," Brenda said. "I told her nobody would be able to figure it out, but she didn't care. She loves Anna, so Anna it had to be. And you have to admit her Victorian dress is beautiful. She rented it from a costume supplier."

"If there's any prize for 'most revealing' tonight, Heather and Peter will have to fight it out," Woody observed. "So it'll just depend on whether the judges are male or female."

As Woody spoke, they noticed Heather walking quickly to the rear of the store, where Bart had just come out of the workroom with Phoebe. He gave Heather his famous grin and stopped to talk to her, admiring the dress. Phoebe, looking exasperated, walked on by them with the bucket of ice she was carrying to the food table. She was tempted to drop it right in front of them just to start a commotion and keep them apart. But before she had a chance, Michael came up and put an arm around her and gave her a kiss.

In the workroom at the rear of the store, Sasha studied herself critically in the small bathroom mirror. She looked like she had stepped out of the Roaring Twenties, with her low-waisted white silk dress tied with a wide bright pink sash and her long string of pearls.

She wished Rob would hurry up and come. It had been several weeks since she had seen him, and she was so anxious for his arrival that she had become irritable and jumpy. She was distracted trying to talk to her friends. All she could think about was that at any moment he would walk through the door.

She left the bathroom and carried several large bottles of soda to the food table, then checked the tape deck. It would take Rob three hours to drive to Rose Hill from his college dorm. If he had gotten off work on time, he should be here by now.

Oh, well, she would just have to stop thinking about him. He'd be there soon.

Several minutes later as she was talking to Chris, she felt two hands go over her eyes. She turned and was in Rob's arms. "I didn't see you come in," she cried excitedly. "I've been watching and watching!"

She stepped back to look at him. With his beard, he looked much older than the other boys at the party. He was dressed in a pure white suit, white shirt, white necktie, and white shoes and socks. Sasha thought he was the most handsome guy in the room.

She pulled him behind one of the high bookcases. "I've missed you so much!" she sighed, throwing her arms around his neck.

"And I've missed you," he said, gently kissing her. "I haven't seen a college girl yet who could hold a candle to you." He stroked her hair and held her tightly, then kissed her again.

"Hi, Chris," Ted said, coming up next to her at the food table. "Nice party, huh?"

Chris smiled at him. "Sure is. I like your outfit. You're skinnier than Babe Ruth, but the uniform looks authentic."

"I won't be skinny if I keep eating these," he said, taking a candy bar from his pocket and popping it into his mouth. "My uncle collects old uniforms. This is one of his."

Chris excused herself, left him, and went over to where Greg stood talking to Peter and Monica. Ted watched her go and sighed heavily. Even though he knew his breakup with Chris had been for the best, sometimes he longed for her stable influence and steady companionship.

As he stood there, he noticed John Marquette lurking outside. Curious, Ted watched out the window as John stood by his car, taking a long drink from a flask. Ted's eyes narrowed. He knew John hadn't been invited. He'd have to alert Sasha and try to keep John out. He was bound to cause trouble.

Kim and Woody approached Ted. "What's so interesting out there, Ted?" Woody asked, following Ted's gaze out the window. "Uh-oh," he said when he saw what was going on. "Looks like Marquette's about to make a grand entrance." But to their surprise, Marquette got in his car and drove away.

"Whew, that's a relief," Kim said. She looked at the groups of people standing around talking. "Looks like things have sort of slowed down. Nobody's dancing. Maybe it's time to do something special."

"Good idea." Woody nodded. "How about starting with girls' choice, to get things started, and make a rule that you can't choose the person you came with."

Kim agreed and went over to stop the music. "Ladies' choice on the next song," she announced loudly, "and you have to pick someone other than your date." She started the music again and moved back to Woody's side. Around them, people began to dance. Phoebe came over and asked Ted, and Brenda grabbed Henry. Fiona had shyly asked Peter. Soon the dance floor was packed.

Kim smiled at Woody. "That was a great idea," she said, giving him a quick kiss on the cheek.

Woody laughed, then stopped suddenly, frowning. Kim followed his eyes and saw Heather pulling Bart onto the dance floor.

Chapter
20

It was already nine-thirty P.M. when Holly parked her car near the bookstore. She hadn't thought she would be so late, but Dr. Ellerbee didn't get back to the clinic as early as he thought he would.

When he arrived, the clinic was quiet. She had spent most of the evening talking to Steve about special scholarships and loans that she might be eligible for. She still wasn't convinced that she would find the necessary money, but she had more than a year before she would start college, so she had plenty of time to investigate various sources of funding.

She mentioned what Bart had told her — that some states had programs to assist students in medical school who would agree to practice medicine in rural areas. Steven was familiar with the program and knew a few students who were participating in it. He said it seemed very worthwhile.

Holly was so happy that she almost had to pinch herself to believe that she wasn't dreaming. Absolutely nothing was going wrong! Suddenly she had a whole new, exciting slant on her future, and the boy of her dreams — the boy she was in love with — seemed to return her feelings. She couldn't wait to get into the bookstore to see him.

She paused at the door to adjust her nurse's cap and the royal blue cape she wore over her starched white uniform. From inside she could hear the plaintive rhythm of one of her favorite songs. She smiled to herself. This would be a perfect song to enter on. She envisioned a romantic encounter. She would walk in, their eyes would meet from opposite ends of the room. He would walk toward her, his eyes never leaving hers, and they would come together on the dance floor.

She felt a shiver go up her spine at the thought. Then she giggled. There wouldn't be any dancing with their arms wrapped around each other — Bart had his left arm in a sling! Well, they'd figure out something.

She took a deep breath and opened the door to the bookstore, trying to adjust her eyes to the dim lights. She could see couples dancing together, most of them hardly moving to the slow, sensuous music. As she looked around, trying to spot Bart, Phoebe came up to her.

"Hi!" she smiled, hugging Holly. "It's about time you got here."

"Phoebe, you look great," Holly said, looking

her over. "I'd know Pippi Longstocking anywhere. You and I used to read those books together in my treehouse — remember? What's wrong, Pheeb? You feel okay? You look sort of upset."

"I'm okay," Phoebe answered, a little too brightly. She quickly drew Holly over to the refreshment table. "Here. Try some of Kim's Havarti cheese dip. It's one their catering business gets lots of requests for."

"Hey!" Holly laughed as she pushed away the cracker and cheese Phoebe was trying to get her to eat. "What's going on! I want to find Bart!"

"Well, just wait a minute. There's plenty of time," Phoebe said, her eyes darting around nervously.

Holly drew back and grinned at her. "Phoebe, what's going on?"

"Nothing," Phoebe said innocently. "Here. Have a stuffed mushroom. They're delicious."

"No thanks," protested Holly. "I just want to find Bart." She glanced around at the couples slow-dancing to the soft music. Sasha and Woody floated by and behind them were Fiona and Peter. Holly glanced through the space between them and thought she saw Bart. She looked closer while Phoebe tried to distract her with food.

Then she saw them. Bart's back was to her. Heather, with her elaborate hairdo and red velvet dress, was dancing with him, one hand holding his, one arm wrapped around his arm in the sling. She was smiling, her face tilted up to his.

Holly immediately looked away, tears stinging

her eyes. "I'm sorry, Holly," Phoebe murmured. "We just had a girls' choice dance and Heather asked Bart to dance. You arrived at the worst time possible."

"Or maybe the best," Holly said under her breath. She tried to collect her thoughts, her mind in a muddle. She looked at Phoebe again, and saw her frantically signaling to someone. "What are you doing?"

"Nothing," Phoebe said innocently.

Holly turned back to the dance floor and saw Ted stopping Bart and pointing to her. Bart quickly turned around, but Holly didn't wait to see his expression. Before Phoebe could stop her, she rushed out the front door. Behind her she heard Bart call, "Holly! Wait!" A moment later she was running down the sidewalk, tears streaming down her face.

When he caught up with her, he grabbed her with his one good arm and pulled her to a stop. She refused to look at him. "What's wrong?" he asked, his voice full of concern.

"Go away! I don't want to talk to you!"

"Holly," he said gently, "if the problem is Heather, I was only dancing with her because there wasn't any way out of it. It was girls' choice."

"There's always a way," Holly said angrily, still refusing to look at him.

"What am I supposed to do if a girl asks me to dance?" he asked pleadingly.

"Say no. It's very simple: N-O."

"That wouldn't be polite," he said.

"Then say yes. Do what you always do and say yes to everyone. Don't change anything for me," she said vehemently, sparks in her eyes.

"I don't believe this. You're jealous." He started to laugh.

"Bart," she said intently, "there's a fine line between flirtation and friendliness. You cross it too often. I don't have any claim on you, but you do act like you care about me, and when you flirt, I'm hurt. It's like a slap in the face to me. What bothers me most is your blindness. You don't *see* what you're doing."

He opened his mouth to say something, then stopped. There was a long pause. He shuffled from one foot to the other. Holly faced him, her expression defiant. "You're right," he said at last, his broad shoulders drooping.

He slouched down on a nearby bench, his right hand rubbing his sore left shoulder. Holly waited. She knew her words had stung him and it pained her to think she had hurt him, but she couldn't apologize. What she had told him was the truth.

Bart shifted his weight on the bench and looked up at her. "I never realized it before. I guess I'm always trying to live up to the image other people have of me, so I do what I think is expected. A lot of girls have this — expectation of me, so I go along with it. I know what you're talking about and I can see that it's hurt you."

He stood up and walked over to her. "Holly," he said very softly, "I like you better than any girl I've ever known." He put his hand gently on her shoulder and drew her close. "And you know what else? I love you."

Holly was certain that her heart had stopped beating. She looked at him, tears still in her eyes. "Bart — " she began.

"I mean it, Holly Daniels. I love you."

As Holly slowly reached out to wrap her arms around his waist, the anger she had felt melted away. She rested her head against his chest and he put his good arm around her, running his fingers through her hair. They stood for a moment in silent communion, and then their lips met gently. Holly moved her arms up to Bart's neck, pulling him even closer, and they kissed again and again, each kiss deeper and more passionate than the last. With each kiss, too, Holly felt her feelings for Bart intensifying, and it felt so good she thought that she could never be apart from him.

When they separated at last, Holly still had tears in her eyes. "I love you, too, Bart," she said softly, smiling at him. And she knew when she said it that it was true.

Without a word they began walking, their locked hands swinging between them. "I can hardly believe this is happening to me," Bart said, a huge smile on his face. He stopped to look at her, his eyes wide with wonder, and kissed her tenderly on the cheek. "You're so beautiful, Holly." He stroked her cheek with the back of his hand, then placed a finger under her chin and tilted her head back so he could kiss her once more. "And you make a gorgeous Catherine Barkley," he said when they started walking again. "After you told me you were coming to the party as Catherine Barkley, I went out and bought *A Farewell to Arms*. I was going to wait until I finished it to tell you, but I'm almost done. I'm enjoying it."

Holly laughed. "What a coincidence. I've been trying to find a copy of *Shane* and read it to surprise *you*." She gazed at him with delight. "I'd tell you how handsome you look tonight in your buckskin shirt and cowboy hat, but Heather's probably already done that, and I wouldn't want it to go to your head." She gave him an impish grin.

"I get the message." He laughed sheepishly.

Holly felt as though she was floating on a cloud. She was so happy to know that Bart returned her feelings and she was relieved that they had finally been able to talk about his flirting.

"Diana and I talked about our folks tonight," Bart said as they began to retrace their steps to the bookstore. "I told her some of the things you said about parents needing to live their own lives and how kids aren't to blame for what happens and can't change anything. She knows it's true. She didn't say any more about how our behavior would make them stay together. I think things will be better now."

"I hope so," Holly said sympathetically. Her voice was suddenly shy. "I talked to Steven tonight at work about medical school. He told me that lots of good scholarships are out there and that if I keep my grades up, I'll be able to qualify for something. He even knew about the program you were telling me about in Montana — the one that encourages medical students to practice in rural areas. So, who knows? Maybe I'll end up a doctor yet, thanks to you."

"You would have decided on your own before long," Bart said. "Know what? I think I've been misreading my father. Di told me that he might be real pleased to learn I want to run the ranch. I'm going to talk to him about it this weekend."

"And the University of Montana?"

"That, too." He looked at her. "But at least it's still almost a year off. I wouldn't want to leave you so soon now that I've found you."

Holly sighed.

"Let's go back to the party," Bart suggested before Holly could say anything. "There are some amazing costumes."

"Great! Let's go!"

"But first," he whispered, drawing her close, "one more kiss. . . ."

Chapter
21

Phoebe sighed happily. "Just look at them, Michael. Aren't they perfect together?"

Michael watched Bart and Holly dancing cheek to cheek and grinned. "Perfect," he said. "They're just like us — they only have eyes for each other. They don't even know that Heather is glaring at them." He put an arm around Phoebe and kissed her tenderly.

"I saw that!" Woody said, coming up to them. "It's elementary, my dear Watson," he said to an imaginary companion as he motioned to Phoebe and Michael, "these two obviously don't like each other very much."

Phoebe giggled and gave Woody a warm hug. "What a brilliant detective you are, Sherlock Holmes. And tell me, are you all ready to act as our master of ceremonies while we give out the costume prizes?" She handed him a folded piece of paper. "Our three anonymous judges have turned in their choices. Here's the list of winners, so I guess it's time."

"Time for what?" asked Kim, coming up to them. "Time for another girls' choice dance? I've had a couple of people ask me about one."

"Let's do that first, then hand out the prizes," Phoebe suggested as the others agreed.

Woody had no sooner announced the girls' choice dance than Heather bounced over to Bart and held out her hand to him. "My turn," she said with sugary sweetness.

Bart hesitated only an instant. "Sorry, Heather." He smiled at her, but none of the old flirtation was in his expression. "I'm spoken for."

Heather's mouth tightened into a pouty expression. "The rules don't work that way. If I ask you, you're supposed to dance with me."

"Bart's right — he's spoken for," Holly said quietly.

Heather looked defiantly at them both. Then she turned her back, an angry expression on her face, signaled to her girl friend to follow her, and without speaking to anyone else, walked out of the bookstore.

Kim saw Heather go and turned worriedly to Woody as the music for the girls' choice dance was starting. "If she tells her mother she had a lousy time, her mother will probably spread bad news about our business."

Woody tried to reassure her. "If she's that petty, there's nothing you can do about it. Your mom will understand that."

Kim was unconvinced. "I hope so," she

frowned, "but I sure hate for her to lose business."

Diana and Jeremy, their arms around each other, walked over to them. "Why so glum, Kim?" Diana asked. "It's been a great party."

"Really a smash," Jeremy agreed. "You and your mother made incredible hors d'oeuvres. Now that my mother has arrived from England, my parents will probably hold some big receptions at the Embassy. I'm going to tell them about Earthly Delights."

"Really?" Kim smiled. "That would be terrific, Jeremy!" She turned to Diana. "Your brother and Holly sure seem to be getting along well."

Diana grinned. "Yeah, I've noticed. It would be impossible not to. They haven't stopped looking at each other since they walked back in. I think it's great."

"Do you think Fiona's having a good time?"

"I do. I think she's starting to like it here quite well," Jeremy replied. "Everyone's been remarkably friendly."

"Okay, everybody, it's time for the prizes," Kim said, moving away from them. "There's Phoebe. Does anyone see Sasha? I'll probably have to go drag her out from behind the bookcase where she's spent practically the whole evening with Rob. I guess they're making up for lost time. Woody, why don't you start the announcements? I'll go get the prizes."

Woody nodded and stopped the tape. "Listen up, gang, time to announce the winners!" he said. Everyone gathered around expectantly.

"Lacey," he said to Peter, "we probably should

have you doing this since you're the voice of Kennedy High, but since I'm playing the greatest detective in literature tonight, it's only right that I snoop out the names and announce them."

He cleared his throat dramatically. "Our prizes tonight are heavenly — all compliments of Rose Hill's finest catering service, Earthly Delights." As everyone cheered, Woody continued, "Our categories are 'truest to character,' 'most obscure,' 'most elaborate costume,' and 'sweepstakes.' We'll start with 'most elaborate.' The winner is — Heather Richardson, splendid in red velvet, as Scarlett O'Hara."

A few people clapped halfheartedly. Woody cleared his throat again, and shrugged his shoulders. "Heather was feeling cold in her dress and had to leave, so we'll make sure she gets her prize later — a half-dozen of Earthly Delights' famous lemon tarts." He opened the box Kim handed him to show off the miniature tarts. There were "oohs" and "aahs" from the crowd.

"Next, the winner of the 'most obscure' category is — Holly Daniels," Woody said with a flourish. "Holly, few of us had heard of that tragic heroine Catherine Barkley, but you're doing wonders for the sales of the book *A Farewell to Arms*, and we assure you that bookstore owners throughout the community of Rose Hill are grateful to you."

Blushing, Holly made her way to Woody's side. He handed her a foil-wrapped box and she opened it to find a half-pound of Earthly Delights' peanut-butter fudge. "Thanks," she said.

She looked around at the faces smiling at her and knew that they were now the faces of friends and that this crowd was her crowd.

"Something tells me I'm going to be a very popular person for the next five minutes," she joked. As everyone clapped, she made her way back to Bart, who promptly popped a piece of the candy into his mouth, then gave her a quick kiss.

Woody put up a hand for quiet. "That brings us to 'truest to character,' a dubious category in which the winner has been picked on the basis of impersonating a literary character he or she is most like. This was a tough one." He consulted his list again. "We've awarded a winner and an honorable mention," he said. "Honorable mention goes to none other than Ted Mason, who occasionally aspires to becoming a professional baseball player and came to the party tonight as Babe Ruth. Ted, even though you're not the world's greatest baseball player — or even Kennedy High's greatest baseball player — everybody thanks you for the candy bars you handed out. They were obviously meant to bribe the judges — and they worked!" he quipped.

Ted good-naturedly came forward and opened his prize, a dozen chocolate eclairs, and immediately began to eat one. "Anybody here want a temporary job as a body guard?" he joked.

"First place in our 'truest to character' goes to — ta-da! Drum roll, please!" Woody waited until the room was totally quiet. "The winner," he grinned, "is none other than Miss Phoebe Hall, who is impersonating everyone's favorite childhood heroine, Pippi Longstocking. Phoebe — will you please come forward?"

Everyone clapped as Phoebe, her red braids bouncing, walked over to Woody. "Miss Longstocking, here is your prize," he said grandly, handing her a gift-wrapped box. Phoebe giggled as she opened it. Inside was one of Earthly Delights' famed Mississippi Mud Cakes. When Phoebe saw it, her green eyes grew very large and she immediately shut the box. "I think I need to go home right now," she said, rolling her eyes in pleasure. "I'm having a chocolate attack and I need a fix."

As Phoebe walked back to Michael, the precious box in her hands, Woody tapped on the edge of the table with his pipe to quiet everyone again. "And now for our grand prize, the sweepstakes award for best overall costume," he said loudly, "I'd like to request that Tweedledum and Tweedledee come here!"

Clapping and cheering, everyone parted as Diana and Jeremy linked arms, assumed idiotic grins, locked their knees, spread their feet wide, and shuffled forward.

"I'm pleased to accept this award," Jeremy said in his munchkin voice.

"Ditto," replied Diana in hers, and the two of them turned to each other and bowed, making everybody crack up.

"Let's open it together," they said at once, as they fumbled with the box. It contained one of Earthly Delights' best creations, Almond Mocha

Cheesecake. They rubbed their fat bellies and licked their lips. As the crowd howled in laughter, they linked arms again, and walked away.

"That's it for the awards, folks," Woody said. "A very special thanks from all of us, Sasha, to you and your parents for allowing you and Phoebe and Kim to have tonight's party here at the Albatross. Now, one more dance and then we all turn into Halloween pumpkins!"

Everyone began to talk, gathering around the winners to see and taste their prizes. As Bart and Holly approached Diana and Jeremy, John Marquette came bursting through the door. "Hey, everyone, having a good time? Sorry I missed it." He turned to face Bart. "Einerson," he said, his words slightly slurred from alcohol, "how's the old shoulder?" He leered at Holly. "Looks like it gets you lots of attention from little nursie here. Maybe I'll do you a favor the next time we're playing and break it for you."

By this time, everyone had stopped dancing and started watching. There was complete silence except for the music as everyone stared in disbelief. Holly gasped as John shoved Bart's injured shoulder. Bart stood his ground. "Wouldn't that be adding insult to injury since you're the one who jumped on me and caused this?" He pointed to his shoulder. His voice was strong and steady. "Whatever games Kennedy loses this season, you can take personal responsibility for, Marquette. Between your pranks and your unsportsmanlike conduct on the field, you're getting a lot of your own teammates sidelined and you're really hurting the rest of us."

Ted stepped next to Bart. "He's right, Marquette. In fact, it wouldn't be a bad idea for the coach to bench you for the season. Maybe some of us should suggest that to him."

John started to lunge at Ted, but the others grabbed him. John struggled, but he couldn't move.

"Get out of here, Marquette," Bart said firmly, standing shoulder to shoulder with Ted. "Nobody invited you here."

"Some people," Ted said, glaring at John, "never learn. Bullies like you won't be able to get away with hurting your own team members *or* the opposition. And you really ought to stop crashing our parties, too. Now get out of here, Marquette."

"I'll get you for this," John mumbled to Ted as he headed toward the door. "You *and* your cowboy friend."

Sasha closed the door behind him and turned to the quiet crowd. "Let's not waste the music, everybody. There's one more dance. Everyone grab your favorite partner." She smiled. "Let's end this night on a happy note!"

Peter, who was standing by the tape deck, put on a soft, melodious love song, and Sasha lowered the lights to the dimmest level. She turned and walked into Rob's arms and they began to dance. Other couples quickly followed — Janie and Henry, Peter and Monica, and then Diana and Jeremy, who for this final dance took the pillows out of their stomachs so they could get really close.

When the music ended, the crowd quietly dispersed, leaving Sasha, Phoebe, and Kim, and their boyfriends, to clean up. One couple remained on the dance floor, standing close together, gazing into each other's eyes. "Hey, Holly! Bart! Party's over," Woody called to them.

They smiled at him, and hand in hand went out the door, thanking the girls for a wonderful time. Outside, under the clear, starlit sky, Bart bent to kiss Holly's nose, cheeks, and finally her mouth. She closed her eyes and gave in to the wave of happiness rushing over her.

"Oh, Bart, I'm so happy," she whispered, her eyes shining.

"So am I," he said softly, his voice full of emotion as he nuzzled her neck with his lips. "I love you, Holly."

"And I love you," she whispered back, her arms holding him tightly. "And I hope we'll be together for a long, long time."

Coming soon . . .
Couples No. 16
SWEETHEARTS

Marc opened the door of Ted's MG, climbed over the bucket seat on the passenger side, and settled down with a thump on the flat space behind the driver's seat. With his long legs folded beneath him, he leaned back on the palms of his hands and watched Dee get in after him.

"It's a little snug. But safe," Marc said. He reached out to hold Dee's hand and steady her as she climbed over the seat. The cold metal of the trunk felt like ice when she sat down.

"It's going to be a bit nippy," Fiona said, her British accent as crisp as the autumn weather.

Dee pulled her sweater a little tighter around her.

"Are you cold?" Marc asked her.

"A little."

"Here." He took off his letter jacket and draped it around her shoulders. She could feel the soft wool against her neck.

171

"Are you sure you don't need it?" Dee asked.

"The cold doesn't bother me. I'm part polar bear."

Dee felt a strange combination of excitement and shyness at finding herself in this unexpected situation, sitting next to a very cute boy who was practically a stranger. Well, this would be a chance to get to know him better, she told herself.

"How come I haven't met you at school before?" Marc asked.

"I moved to Rose Hill less than a year ago."

Dee didn't want to explain that she used to be chubby and he probably had seen her but didn't recognize her now. Instead she said, "It takes a while to get to know people in a school as big as Kennedy."

A gust of wind blew Dee's short hair out of place. Marc gently pushed it back from her forehead. The gesture seemed so natural, but it was so intimate that Dee felt a little awkward.

Another gust of wind came up, and Dee shivered again.

"Are you still cold?" Marc asked.

Dee nodded. "I guess I'm *not* part polar bear," she said, rubbing her cold hands together.

"Hold my paw! It'll warm you up." Marc laughed again and took her hand in his, his blue eyes twinkling. Dee wasn't about to tell him, but the minute he took her hand she really did feel warm all over.